Father's
Arcane Daughter

OTHER YEARLING BOOKS YOU WILL ENJOY:

Father's
Arcane Daughter
by
E. L. Konigsburg

A YEARLING BOOK

Published by
Dell Publishing Co., Inc.
1 Dag Hammarskjold Plaza
New York, New York 10017

Yearling ® TM 913705, Dell Publishing Co., Inc.

ISBN: 0-440-42496-8

Printed in the United States of America

September 1986

10 9 8 7 6 5 4 3 2 1

CW

For my good friend,
WINSTON ELLIOT CARMICHAEL,
and she knows why.

Father's
Arcane Daughter

one

Later—much, much later—when we both knew what we had bought and what it had cost, she said that I should tell it.

"But," I protested, "there are some parts that I hardly know and other parts that I don't know at all."

She smiled. "Life's like that. A little knowing. A lot of not knowing."

"My telling will be a string of incidents. Like the separate frames of a comic strip. Besides," I said, "I'm bound to give myself all the good lines."

"A mood can be an incident," she said.

"Oh, no!" I protested. "No, no, no, no, no. Moods are colors."

"The comic strips are colored on Sundays. And in books."

I thought a minute. "For me it all began on a Thurs-
day, a September Thursday in 1952."

"Begin it there," she urged. "That Thursday is a good
place to begin. It is precise. You'll see, the rest will fol-
low."

IT WAS EASY to remember which day of the week it
began because Thursday was a particular wart in my
week.

It was early day at Wardhill Academy, which by it-
self was good, but it was also early day at Holton Progressive, Heidi's school, and that was bad. Our mother
always went to the beauty parlor on Thursdays, and
with Mother gone, it became my responsibility to amuse
Heidi. And that was what actually made Thursday the
most disagreeable day of the week.

Heidi sat at the table in the breakfast room, waiting.
She watched while I ate the snack that Cora had prepared. She sat there, her head propped on her hand, her
elbow on the table and asked, "What'll we do today,
Winston?"

I knew the question would come. Once a week it
came, and I waited for it, the way I waited for the bell
changing classes—with a mixture of expectation and
dread. I never answered immediately. She watched my
face for an answer, and I waited until she turned aside
and then I said, in a quiet monotone, in tones I knew
she could not hear, "Why don't you go into the kitchen
and have Cora teach you how to do two things at once,

4

my dear? Like putting your head in the oven and turning on the gas?"

Heidi turned back, "Did you say something?" I chewed on my brownie, looking straight at her. I said nothing, and she got tired of watching my lips in motion, not making words. "Mummy says . . ." she began.

I stopped chewing. "Why don't you call our mother, *Mother?*" I asked. I looked at her and added, "A mummy is something all stiff and wrapped in bandages."

"But Mummy sounds cozier."

I chewed on the brownie some more and took a swig of milk. Cora was one of our better cooks. I hoped she would stay. The cook before Cora had lasted six months, and the one before that had lasted seven meals; she had quit after breakfast on the third day. No wonder. With Heidi around, it was like cooking for two different households on one salary.

Heidi leaned closer, she was watching my lips, not wanting to miss the moment when my chewing would change into talking. I opened my mouth, a huge moosh of chocolate, nuts and milk and made a gargling sound. It was a quiet gargle, and its sound—effectively repulsive, I thought—was lost on Heidi. She just stared at my maw, waiting, watching, leaning over, not wanting to miss anything I might say.

"Look," I said at last, speaking slowly now so she could easily read from my lips those sounds she couldn't hear, "Let me finish my snack. Let me go upstairs, and let me take care of certain important body functions. Let me also change my clothes. Let me do all those

5

things out of sight of you, and I'll play the Invisible Game."

I watched Heidi smile that warm, wet, creature smile of hers, and then she larrupped away. I liked the word *larrup*, it suited her; water buffaloes larrup, and so do hyenas. I had accumulated a secret vocabulary of words that applied just to Heidi's queer, bumpy ways.

I could see her waiting in the library as I passed by on my way to my room. In her lap were her gatherings for the game. I hung up my school blazer; the school year was new enough that it had not yet become short in the sleeves, but old enough to have one soup stain and one small spaghetti. I did everything I had told Heidi I would do, and when I couldn't drag things out any longer, I went downstairs to face my Thursday fate: fun and games with Heidi.

The Invisible Game was her favorite. The chief rule was that everything was invisible to everyone except Heidi. *Everyone* really meant me, for I was the only one who ever played with her. I was blindfolded and seated at the far end of the library. Losing the full use of one of my senses made me Heidi's equal. Heidi brought me things to identify. Each item was given a value, depending on its difficulty. If an article had a value of three, and I identified it correctly, I was permitted to take three blindfolded steps out of the library. If I bumped into a piece of furniture, I had to take double that number of steps back. Once I made it to the door, the game was over.

She was clever at finding things hard to identify. She

gathered them from all over the house. A toenail clipper, a napkin ring, a single cuff link, a lace-paper doily.

On that Thursday I had advanced through toilet paper roller and paper punch when the doorbell rang. Partly out of annoyance—I had in my hand a tiny dress snap, which I couldn't identify—and partly out of a need to assert myself, I tore off my blindfold and ran to the door.

Heidi screamed, "Winston, W-I-N-S-T-O-N," and came running after me.

I managed to flick on the switch of the intercom and ask, "Who is it?" when Heidi arrived in the foyer and in her rage espaliered herself against the black and white marble floor and bit my ankle. I screamed, and the voice at the other end of the intercom called, "What's happened? What's the matter?"

I couldn't tell that voice that what was really the matter was that I had broken a cardinal rule of the Invisible Game, Heidi's Game. I had allowed myself to use all of my senses.

The person at the door jiggled the door knob just as Simmons, who had heard the remote in the kitchen, reached the foyer. He switched off the intercom with his right hand and picked Heidi up in his left arm and deposited her a knight's move away from my foot. He then switched the intercom back on and asked in a voice as cool as autumn rain, "Who is it, please?"

"Is everything all right?" the voice asked.

"May I help you?" Simmons responded.

"Is someone injured?" the voice insisted.

7

"Everything is fine, thank you," Simmons answered. "How may I help you?"

"I am here to see Mr. Carmichael."

"He is not in at the moment. Did you have an appointment?"

"No."

"I suggest that you call his office and arrange an appointment."

And then, as if the person were at the other end of a telephone not the other side of a door, Simmons asked, "Whom may I say is calling, please?"

"This is Caroline."

There was no further voice at the other end of the intercom. I heard footsteps, and I hobbled over to the parlor window, listing starboard, rubbing my ankle.

I saw the back of a tall, thin lady as she walked toward a taxi. She had a lighted cigarette in her hand. I watched her raise her hand toward her mouth and take a puff. Only in detective movies had I ever seen a woman walking and smoking a cigarette at the same time. The woman walked toward a waiting taxi.

I moved from the window and looked over at Heidi and saw her upper lip fold over her lower like living sponge. I was glad that she had bitten my ankle. She had not called for Luellen, and I knew she wouldn't tell Mother that I had tried to answer the door.

MOTHER RETURNED HOME, wearing a yellow scarf over her hair. The scarf was made of a thin material and was just long enough to tie under her chin.

She sat down on the ottoman in the library and Heidi

climbed, amoebalike, onto her lap. The knot of the yellow scarf was tight, and its working ends were short. Heidi's fingers tugged and pulled. Mother sat there, wearing a smile like a cosmetic, as Heidi unwrapped her Mummy.

Mother lifted Heidi off her lap. Small though she was for ten, she was still half her life past the stage where she would be sitting on laps, cuddling. Mother's skirt looked like a cafeteria serving of tuna casserole.

She got up from the ottoman, and I watched as she brushed at her dress, and then I asked her if she were finished.

"Finished what?" she asked.

"Finished being patient."

Mother rushed a worried glance over toward Heidi, and I could read her look of relief when she realized that Heidi hadn't heard. I had deliberately spoken softly.

"What do you want?" Mother asked.

"Caroline came today," I said.

"Caroline who?"

"I have no idea. Came in a taxi."

"In a taxi? What did she look like?"

"I saw only her back and her right profile. She was smoking."

"Well, if it was anything important, she'll come back. Did Simmons get her last name? Never mind, I'll ask him myself." She was walking away. I could tell she was anxious to get upstairs to change her clothes.

*   *   *

9

THAT EVENING the doorbell rang.

Mother and Father were sitting in the library. Father had already had his brandy, smoked his cigar and had returned to his desk. Heidi was in bed. That would make it past nine thirty, late for someone to be calling.

I had been in my room reading *Junior Scholastic*, an assignment, but I could never resist the call of a doorbell, so I folded the magazine and started downstairs. I saw Simmons scurrying across the foyer floor. His movements were usually as glossy as Mother's hair on Thursday afternoons.

By racing, Simmons managed to keep ahead of the woman and arrive at the library door first. There was enough time for him to say, "Mr. Carmichael, there is a Miss Caroline to see you," and there was enough time for Father to look up from his papers before the woman arrived at the archway and said, "Hello, Father, I'm home."

I could not see her face, but I saw Father grow pale. The woman turned to Mother and said, "I see that you've replaced the oriental rugs with wall-to-wall carpeting."

Recognition dawned on Mother. "Caroline! You're Caroline!" she said.

Father remained speechless.

The woman nodded.

Father got up from his desk and walked quickly but quietly across the room. He took the woman by the shoulders. I could see his face, not hers. He looked intensely—even fiercely—into her eyes. Then he pulled her to him and hugged her, and her arms left her sides for the first time. She returned his embrace.

Mother sent Simmons out of the room and closed the heavy doors that sealed the library off from the hall and effectively sealed me off from the life in the library.

two

"Didn't you suspect who Caroline was?" she asked.

"Of course I suspected. That made me more anxious to hear the story firsthand. I wanted to be told. I wanted to be included."

"Included in what?" she asked.

"Included in the past. I had always known that Caroline was the shadow under which I was growing up. I wanted, at last, to learn the shape of that shadow."

"Did you think that once defined, it would disappear?" she asked.

"I thought that it would grow smaller when exposed to full light. Shadows are supposed to."

BREAKFAST WAS as usual the next morning. Mother appeared in the breakfast room just as Luellen was helping

12

Heidi gather her things together. Mother always came down to check if Heidi had all her equipment. Heidi never carried books to Holton Progressive; she always carried things. That day it was flour, paper clips and sandpaper.

Mother skimmed a look at me and asked if I had everything I needed. But that was just courtesy. I never forgot anything.

I waited until Heidi's back was turned before I said softly, "I want to talk to you about last night."

Mother's head tilted up suddenly as if I had landed a light jab. "What about last night?"

"Caroline," I answered. Then I turned and walked out. Maurice was holding open the door to the back seat. I ignored the courtesy and opened the front door and slid in. Maurice didn't like that, and Mother didn't, either.

"Why aren't you riding in the back with Heidi?"

"I'm allergic to flour dust."

"Since when?"

"Since last week—last week she brought flour to school three times," I threw out my hands. "Overexposure did it."

Heidi waved "bye-bye"—she always called it that—and Mother blew kisses to both of us. I never waved nor blew.

AFTER SCHOOL I wasted no time. I tracked Mother down even before taking a snack. I told her that I wanted to see her alone to discuss the matter I had mentioned that morning.

13

"I called your Father about that," she said. "He wants to speak to you about it after dinner."

I suddenly felt like a prime minister. Father would tell me. He would explain. Father would tell me everything I needed to know. As I ate my crumb cake, Mrs. Wylie, our cleaning lady, passed through the breakfast room. "Winston," she said, "I wish I felt about Fridays the way you look."

I answered, "Not every Friday."

I DID NOT ONCE mention Caroline all through dinner. I made no effort to rush through the meal, and when dinner was over, I hesitated long enough to allow Mother and Heidi to be the first out of the dining room. They crossed the foyer toward the library, and I hung back, waiting to take whichever direction Father did.

He headed toward the library. I caught up with him and said, "Father . . ."

"Yes, Winston?"

"Have you forgotten our discussion?"

"Not at all." He held out his arm, ushering me toward the library.

"But Heidi and Mother are in there."

"Yes. Your mother thinks it best that Heidi be told, too." He glanced down and studied my face. "I'm sure you would prefer it that way." Father was not telling me what I *would* prefer; Father was telling me what I *should* prefer.

Mother was holding a scrapbook when I walked into the library. She clutched it to her breast with both arms.

14

It filled all the space from the crook of one arm to the crook of the other.

Father began. It was necessary that he speak slowly and face Heidi to make certain that she could follow:

Seventeen years ago, Father's daughter, Caroline, had left home to go to college in Philadelphia, a small exclusive girl's school, not known for its academic excellence but for the fact that nice girls went there. In the spring of a brief freshman year, she made reservations to fly home for vacation. She never arrived. She never reached the airport. The taxi driver was one of three men who kidnapped her.

The kidnappers demanded that the rich and famous Mr. Charles Carmichael give them half a million dollars. He was allowed to talk to Caroline on the phone after he reassured the men that he would not notify the police, mark the bills (they wanted to be paid in cash), and that he would make no effort to track them down.

"But a person can be very wealthy and have very little money on hand. A person cannot put an ad in the classified section of the paper and sell a mill making factory equipment. In short, there is no way for even a very rich man to get his hands on five hundred thousand dollars cash without others getting involved. Over a period of a week, the kidnappers called three times. The first two times they allowed me to speak to Caroline. Then, the third time they called, the time when we were to arrange for the pickup, they wouldn't allow me to speak to her. They said that they had moved her. I asked for some reassurance that she was still alive, and they told me that I would have that the following day, that two hours after they had picked up the money, I would receive another call telling me where Caroline could be found.

"That call was traced, and the police staked out the place from which it was made. The police agreed to allow me to pay the ransom; they did not want to endanger Caroline's life. But when one of the men, probably en route to picking up the ransom, spotted someone, he returned to the house. Once inside, he fired a high-powered rifle and killed the policeman. Then there were further shots from the house, and finally the police began returning fire. It turned into an old-fashioned shoot-out.

"The house was an old frame house outside of Latrobe. We don't know what started the fire—whether the men inside, realizing the hopelessness of the situation, deliberately set it, or whether it was started by the gunfire.

"Four bodies were burned beyond recognition. We were told that one was Caroline's. But I have always had my doubts. That last call, the one when they said that Caroline had been moved—I have always held onto the possibility that she was not in the house. That doubt has been my hope."

"How do you know that the lady who came yesterday is your daughter?" I asked.

Mother answered. "At this moment we aren't certain." She smiled. "At this moment we are quietly checking into the lady's claim. It seems strange to me that she

16

would appear just months before her thirty-fifth birthday, the deadline for her to claim the Adkins inheritance."

I addressed Father, "Aren't there some identifying scars or birthmarks?"

Father smiled, a smile of delight. "The lady has them."

"What about fingerprints?"

"There is no record of fingerprints. There was never any thought of them. My daughter was not a criminal; she was a college student."

"Your father has never given up hope that Caroline would return one day," Mother said. She was still clutching the scrapbook. "Sorrow strengthens some and softens others. Unfortunately, Caroline's mother fell into despair."

"Did she commit suicide?" I asked.

"In an indirect way."

Father shot Mother a glance. "Come right out and say it, Grace." He sighed heavily, wearily. "What your mother is trying to say is that Caroline's mother took to alcohol." He said it very fast, and I didn't know if Heidi caught what he had said. I looked back at Father who seemed to be regretting his small outburst.

Father patted Mother's shoulder. "You see," he said, "something especially good came from that misfortune." He looked at me and Heidi and added, "Your mother. I met your mother because of Anne's drinking. She had come to take care of her." He patted her shoulder again, but it remained stiff. Father walked away, cleared his throat and said, "Anne, Caroline's mother, was a lovely woman in every way. Every other way."

"Where has this Caroline been keeping herself?" I asked.

"Ethiopia," Father answered. "Ethiopia. Working as a nurse."

Father moved to a wing chair, the one with the ottoman. Heidi moved from the sofa where she had been sitting and climbed onto the ottoman and then onto Father's lap. He absentmindedly rubbed his hand through her hair. Heidi waited until he glanced down, and then she said, her lips pursed out, as if she would talk in kisses if she could, "I promise you, Father, that I will never get kidnapped."

Mother smiled. I knew already that the remark would be repeated at the Club and at Mr. Rick's on Thursday. "Heidi, darling, no one ever chooses to be kidnapped," she said.

"What with all the chauffering and chaperoning that goes on around here," I said, "choice or an act of an angry God are the only possible ways it could happen."

Father rubbed his forehead and looked at me. His look was strange—apologetic. "I suppose we have been very, very protective," he said, "but these are dangerous times."

"I understand," I said. I didn't care to carry on the conversation any longer. "May I look at the scrapbook?" I asked.

"It's your mother's."

Yes, I thought, it would be Mother's. Father wouldn't cut and paste details between the covers of a book.

Mother handed it to me, and I carried it up to my room. It was surprisingly heavy. Like carrying half a sister.

I STUDIED that scrapbook. What a wealth of detail I found there. Detail cast under a thousand watt bulb. There was no history more strange to me than the immediate past history of my family.

There had been times when the Golden Age of Greece had seemed closer to me than what had happened to the Carmichaels before I was born. I could more easily fit people into togas than I could the twenties. Even the history book picture of Great-Grandfather Carmichael seated beside Carnegie and Frick seemed more familiar to me than the pictures of Father in the library, like the one that shows him wearing a Princeton football uniform. The uniform is standard in all its essentials, but old fashioned in its details; and those tiny differences always made it more difficult for me to place Father in time.

I began studying the scrapbook by looking for clues. I studied the face of Anne Adkins Carmichael and then the picture of Caroline, which had been in all the papers. I thought that I would enjoy being very clever and finding some small flaw, some small difference that would prove beyond the shadow of a doubt that the woman who said she was Caroline really was—or really was not. But I soon gave up reading in the scrapbook for that kind of information. I began, instead, reading to make myself familiar with my family, particularly my Father, a man both familiar and strange. I knew much about Father's moods and almost nothing about his thinking. I had long been an accurate reader of facial expressions and body language. There was a certain look Father had that said *tired* and a certain tilt to his shoulders that said *busy*. Father said so very little that I had learned to "listen" to his face. I read Father's face for the same reason that Heidi read lips—to know what was really being said.

three

"Did the scrapbook help to give Caroline a shape?" she asked.

"Yes, in a way."

"An important way?"

"Not especially." She looked puzzled. "Let me explain. I said that I had always known that there had been a Caroline. I had always known that Father had been married before and that he had had a daughter named Caroline. I had known it. But I hadn't realized it. Realize in the literal sense. It had never seemed real."

"Would you say, then, the scrapbook made it seem real?"

"No," I answered. "It was the look on Father's face. That glimpse I had had of Father's face that Thursday night before the library door was closed. That look said that there had once been a Caroline, and she had been very loved."

"All that from a glimpse?" she asked.

How could she ask such a question? "When shadows are all he has, a prisoner learns to tell time by the light coming in through a slit under the door," I said. "Facial expressions were primary Carmichael language. English was second."

She smiled and leaned back. "I never really thought it was the scrapbook."

ON THE LAST FRIDAY of October I saw something new in Father's look; something newborn, I thought. Then I realized what it was. Outside the front entrance to our house were two boxwood trees that Solomon, our gardener, kept carefully groomed into pompons. In the spring of the year bright green sprigs kept popping out, destroying their perfectly round margins. Father looked like that; he was sprouting bright green sprigs of joy.

After dinner Father called Heidi and me into the library. He explained: There was now a lot of evidence, and all of it seemed to prove that the woman who claimed to be Caroline really was. She knew dates and details that only someone in the family could have known. No one—not Mother, not the lawyers—had been able to trip her.

"Where has she been?" I asked.

"In Ethiopia," Father answered.

22

"You've mentioned that," I said. "I mean, where has she been staying since that Thursday."

"In an apartment in Sewickley. We have reason to fear that some people are beginning to suspect her real identity, so your mother has kindly suggested that we have her move in with us until all the legal papers are signed. It is important that we avoid publicity." Father paused a minute and then said that he had a selfish request to make; he hoped that both of us would understand. He asked us not to invite any of our playmates (he used the word *playmates*) over to the house for a while, not until all the papers regarding Caroline were signed. After that—after everything was complete and legal—he would make an official announcement to friends, relatives and to the press. Could we understand his need for secrecy?

We both said yes.

I could understand the need for secrecy. From the scrapbook I had seen that Caroline Carmichael had been front page news for two months. All across the United States and in Europe as well. Even on the first anniversary of her disappearance, there had appeared interviews with former high school classmates. No longer on page one, but back on page fourteen were interviews with Beatrice (Bunny) Miller and with Helen Nadel, her classmates at Finchley, saying what a nice person Caroline had been and how they missed her. And there had appeared an interview with Agatha Trollope, the headmistress of Finchley, as well.

So I could understand Father's asking us to keep

Caroline's reappearance a secret. What I couldn't understand was his asking us not to have anyone over to the house. When had we ever had friends (playmates) over? Three years ago, I had. That was my last time.

THREE YEARS AGO I had asked Barney Krupp over for a Saturday afternoon. We couldn't keep Heidi out of the sun-room where we were playing. She sat on the floor in the middle of our game sucking her thumb and watching everything we said. Like some troglodyte. *Troglodyte* was my newest word in my special vocabulary. I wanted her to go. I said to Barney, making certain that Heidi could hear, "Did you sprinkle the powder?"

Barney got my message and answered, "Yes, Win, but are you sure that it will only affect unmarried females?"

I pretended that I didn't want Heidi to hear, all the time making certain that she could, and said, "Yes, Barney; its sensitivity is triggered by the klondestitine hormone found only in unmarried girls."

"And you say that the tips of the fingers are the first to dissolve?"

"Yes, unless the victim sucks her thumb and then, of course, the roof of the mouth goes first. Sometimes the dissolution continues up through the skull, and the girl is left with a hole in her head. That symptom is known as the chimney effect. Can only be disguised by growing the eyebrows extra long and combing them back over the hole."

24

Barney asked, "Did you sprinkle a generous amount all over the room?"

"Every surface."

Heidi took her thumb out of her mouth and rubbed her whole hand over the top of the table, knocking down an ashtray and a vase. She looked at me the whole time she was causing the destruction, and when she was done, she said, "I've touched everything. Everything. And I still have all my fingers." She held up both hands, then said, "I can still do this." She thumbed her nose first at me and second at Barney, sticking out her tongue at the same time.

"C'mon, Barney," I said. We got on either side of her and lifted her out of the room. She was very small and not very heavy, and it was not difficult. I quickly closed the door to the sun-room and since it had no lock, pushed a large chair in front of it.

But Heidi had no talent for being ignored. She sent up such a wallow that Luellen came running. Luellen called for me to open up. But I would not. Heidi screamed at Luellen to *get Mummy, get Mummy*, and Luellen did. Heidi continued screaming until Mother arrived, and Barney and I pushed back the chair and opened the door. Mother was holding Heidi, and Heidi was sucking her thumb. Mother accused me of being selfish and inconsiderate, and when I looked at Heidi, straining to hear what I would say, when I looked at her thumb in her mouth like the stem on a fungus, I worried that Mother might be right.

Barney hardly knew where to look while Mother

scolded, so he looked down at the floor. I realized that he was thinking that he had certainly not done me a favor by coming to visit.

I fell into the habit of not asking anyone over. No one—except possibly Barney—noticed. Only a few of the boys at Wardhill were buddies outside of school. They all came from scattered parts of the city.

Of course, I thought, Father would not have realized that we never had friends over to the house. On Saturdays he was usually absent locally or absent long distance; his Saturdays were spent either at the office or out of town.

On a usual Saturday Heidi and I went to our piano lessons in the morning. We took our lessons at the Convent of the Sacred Heart. Sister Clothilde was our teacher, the best in Pittsburgh according to Mother, and she didn't make house calls.

"Let's take Winston before Hilary," Sister would say. Sister was the only person who called Heidi by her real name, and there in that barren, immaculate classroom, I thought that Heidi, the name, as well as Heidi, the golliwog, was out of place. (I also hoped that such un-Christian thoughts could be neutralized by passing through the walls of the convent.)

Then I waited while Heidi took her lesson. I always carried along a book, but I never opened it. I spent my time wondering about Sister Clothilde. I sat there, my book opened on my lap, and wondered how she could always look so unwrinkled and cool. And how she never smelled. Never smelled of wool gabardine or perspiration or soap or incense or mint or must. Was it because she was pure? Purer than Ivory soap which was only 99 44/100% pure and had a slight but clean odor.

From our piano lessons Maurice drove us to the big Carnegie Library near the University. There we chose books and picked up one of each pamphlet and bookmark that was on the checkout counter. Next we were taken to the Hotel Webster Hall Coffee Shop where I ordered a Devonshire sandwich for myself and a hamburger—no bun and no pickle—for Heidi. After the waitress brought the hamburger, I would request a roll and after that arrived, a small order of french fries. That way I made certain that everything came in separate dishes, for Heidi would eat nothing if one part of her meal touched another. I cut my sister's hamburger into spoon-size pieces, and I knew by the smiles I received from the other patrons of the restaurant that people noticed how thoughtful and kind I was. I wished I could be unaware of the favorable impression I made, or—second best—not enjoy it. I often wondered what kind of a brother I would be if I didn't have to be the kind I was.

The restaurant was never crowded when we were there; we always arrived by 11:00 A.M.; Maurice waited for us in the lobby of the hotel. I always asked the waitress for the check and signed the bill, WINSTON ELLIOT CARMICHAEL, and then added 10% TIP just as I had been taught to do at the Club.

From the Hotel Webster Hall we went to the Hotel Schenley where we both ordered Joyce's cream pie. I cut Heidi's for her, and Maurice waited outside on Fifth

27

Avenue while we ate. The windows of Joyce's were not draped, and Maurice had only to do an about-face to be in full view of us. It never occurred to me that on a cold day, I might hurry over my Joyce's cream pie or that I might skip it altogether. If the thought had ever occurred to me, I squelched it. I needed that part of the week more than Maurice needed to come in from the cold.

Then we went home.

Heidi took a nap, and I read or wrote letters. I often wrote several letters on a Saturday:

Dear Jell-O:

There is no dessert more American than Jell-O, and there is no fruit more American than cranberries. I suggest that you make CRANBERRY your next flavor.

Sincerely,
Winston Elliot Carmichael

Dear Mr. Heyerdahl,

I have just finished reading *Kon Tiki*, and I would like to tell you that I enjoyed the story of your adventures very much. I would like to volunteer for your next expedition. (I am very healthy and extremely good natured.)

Sincerely,
Winston Elliot Carmichael.

28

Dear Mr. Berle,

I saw one of your television programs the other night, and I have a word of advice to you to improve it: RETIRE.

Sincerely,
Winston Elliot Carmichael.

When Heidi woke from her nap, we usually went to a movie. If Mother were home, she drove; if not Maurice drove, and Luellen took us in.

That was my usual Saturday, had been for years. Saturdays were not unpleasant; they had a certain rhythm. We were syncopated, Heidi and I.

four

She sat back in her custom-fitted upholstered chair. "Very good so far," she said.

I was pleased she said that. "Thank you," I said. "You look prepared to take a back seat for a while."

"I've learned to do that."

"You know," I said. "I think that someone who has been in prison resents the person who frees him. Freedom interrupts something very important."

"What?" she asked.

"It interrupts a person's self-absorption."

"You keep making references to prison . . ."

"But, of course, I do. It was that."

"When did you realize that it was?"

"When I got out. If you're raised inside a huge shelter, one that you've never seen from the outside, how *would you know that it was a prison unless you saw it from the outside?"*

"Tell about your first steps outside," she urged.

CAROLINE MOVED IN on the last Tuesday in October. I arrived home from school at the usual time.

"Is she here?" I asked.

"Yes," Mother answered, "she is in her room, resting."

"She only brought one suitcase," Heidi said, "and she isn't very pretty."

I would not say what I was thinking: that someone once long ago had cut the muscles that allowed a compliment to come from Heidi's tongue. Instead I asked, "Did Cora quit?"

"Oh," Mother said. "Is that your way of telling me that you are ready for something to eat? What would you like?"

"Something sweet and chemical and with no nutritional value whatsoever."

"Winston!" Mother scolded. "Are you deliberately trying to provoke me?"

"No, no, my dear," I said raising my eyebrows and twirling an invisible moustache. "You are provocative enough already, you lovely thing you."

Mother laughed out loud. She stepped into the kitchen to tell Cora that I was home. Heidi left with her.

I smiled my thanks to Cora when she brought me a

tray. I ate with my worst possible manners and thought my worst possible thoughts. Another sister! A long-lost brother would be preferable to a long-lost sister. A long-lost kangaroo would be better than either a brother or a sister.

I made up my mind to one thing. I wouldn't start this whole new sister thing by pretending that I liked any part of it. I wouldn't pretend about anything. When she says, How are you? I'll say, Exactly as I ought to be. When she says, (everyone always does!), You resemble your father; I'll say, I should also resemble an ape, being that I am descended from them, too.

At last, having eaten and thought all that was on the menu for the day, I gathered together my books and put my blazer on top of the pile and started up the stairs.

SHE WAS STANDING on the upstairs landing. I saw her over the rim of books.

"Hello," she said. "I'm Caroline. You're Winston, I know."

"Yes, I'm Winston."

"I watched Maurice drive in with you. I've been waiting for you."

"I just, well, I hadn't had much lunch at school today, and I just, well, I just took something to stave off the pangs until dinner."

"I know," she said. "When I lived here, I used to have something to eat when I came home from school." She paused and said nothing more. She was smiling, but she didn't add anything to that. My turn?

"I have your old room," I said.

"I know. I hope you love it as much as I did." Then a pause, friendly enough, but awkward.

My turn again? "You can have it back if you want."

"Please don't bother. As soon as everything is settled, I'll have an apartment of my own."

"It won't be any bother. Honest. You can have your room back tonight if you want."

She laughed. "I probably wouldn't be able to get the gymnasium odor out of it in so short a time."

"Oh," I said. "I'm not especially athletic, and I am very neat."

"Neat," she repeated. Then she looked at me a long time, a very direct, very long look. "Yes, Winston, you are neat. Neat," she repeated. A pause, not as long as the others, and then she added, "Would you call for me so that we can go down to dinner together?" And then she gave me a smile. The smile registered as something special, some new word in my vocabulary of facial expressions. I would have to decide what it was. Maybe it was significant. Maybe it was a clue to her identity.

I nodded. "I'll call for you."

She said, "That, too, will be neat. Very neat."

I went to my room and threw myself across my bed. Stupid, stupid, stupid-o! I had practically begged her to throw me out of my room. Dumb, dumb, dummy-me! I loved my room. I sometimes felt that my room was the best friend I had in the house. What had come over me? Where had I lost control? At what point had I decided to do everything that I had said I wouldn't do?

I took down the scrapbook and studied it. I reread the interviews with Caroline's classmates. They had all agreed that Caroline Carmichael had been a nice person. But nice was not what I would have chosen to describe her, not unless I could qualify nice. Warm nice? Maybe. But something else. Something I had never met with in an adult before. I had to think about it.

THERE WAS A small bouquet of flowers by the place setting across from me, next to Heidi. Caroline picked up the flowers, looked at Father and said, "Thank you. You remembered."

"Remembered what?" Mother asked, looking over at Father. Father paid no attention to Mother.

"Remembered what?" Mother asked again.

"Anemones," Caroline answered. She walked over to the head of the table and kissed Father just below the earlobe. I was shocked. Here was this woman—over thirty—and still allowed to moosh over Father. It was much easier to be a daughter than to be a son.

"I know they're anemones," Mother said. She added a little laugh, it came out as a whimper. "I also know that it's not Caroline's birthday. What *is* the special occasion?"

"My mother would have been fifty-seven today," Caroline said. "She loved anemones."

Mother looked at Father. "That was very thoughtful of you, Charles."

Heidi reached toward the flowers. Mother, who was sitting on Heidi's right, tapped her hand to get her attention and said, "Those are Caroline's. They are very special." She looked up and smiled at Caroline.

34

"I just want to look at them," Heidi said.

"May she hold them?" Mother asked. Her smile changed to the one that people wore for asking unnecessary permissions like, May I help you with your coat?

Caroline said, Of course, and Heidi began to reach for the flowers, her hand open, her arm moving like a broken clutch across the tablecloth. Caroline watched the hand for a minute, and then lifted the flowers herself and handed them to Heidi. Heidi held the small vase as if she were going to drink from it, and some of the water spilled on her lap.

"Give the flowers back to Caroline, darling," Mother said. "They are very special." Heidi returned the flowers, and Grace said, "That's a good girl."

"They don't smell," Heidi said.

Mother lifted the dinner bell, rang it, and dinner was served. Grapefruit first; Heidi had none. She sat, her head propped on her arm, watching Caroline eat. When the main course arrived, Father carved and Simmons carried Heidi's portion into the kitchen, returning with it cut up on Heidi's special divided platter. Heidi put her elbow on the table and propped her head on her hand and began the left-handed, wooly operation that transported food from her plate to her mouth. She ate everything with a spoon even though a full setting of cutlery was put at her place. I watched her as I had not watched her in a long time. She ate with a weird kind of concentration, not like a puppy—all eagerness and appetite—but like some lower form of life, something cenazoic.

Caroline smiled at Father. "Did you request the lamb?" she asked. "We had it often over there."

"No," Father replied. "That touch of thoughtfulness was Grace's. She planned the menu."

Caroline looked at Mother. "Thank you," she said. "It's delicious."

I noticed that Mother looked uneasy. Was it just the strangeness of the situation? No, it was something about Caroline. Was it because she had not shown any enthusiasm about sharing her flowers with Heidi?

"So many people," Mother said, "ignore lamb, except for chops . . ."

At that moment, Heidi's fork appeared from far horizons and jabbed a piece of lamb from Caroline's plate. Caroline who had been looking at Mother saw the motion out of the corner of her eye and jumped back in alarm. "Oh! my God!" she exclaimed. "What was that?"

"Just Heidi," I answered. "She always does that. But it's usually Father's plate."

Heidi's head was still propped on her hand; she was chewing. Mother looked at her and smiled and then looked up at Caroline and gave a gentle, what-can-one-do? shrug.

"I don't like that," Caroline said.

Mother, embarrassed and surprised, replied, "But she is only a child."

"I don't like it," Caroline repeated.

"Surely," Mother said, "your natives in Ethiopa did not all have dainty table manners."

36

"Their behavior at table—when they had a table—was appropriate. One does not expect the manners of a barbarian at a table set with crystal and damask."

Father interrupted, "Surely, Grace, there is no reason . . ."

Mother passed him a glare that withered the rest of his sentence. "Tomorrow," she said, "Caroline can sit with Winston."

"She can sit there now," I suggested.

Heidi's head was still propped on her hand, her elbow still on the table. She was chewing with large semivoluntary movements like the underside of a slug pressed against the glass wall of a terrarium. She had heard almost nothing. She sat like that until she noticed Caroline getting up.

Caroline took her place at my side.

When I was delivered from school the following day, Caroline was waiting for me in the breakfast room. She sat across from me at the table; I barely said hello. What right had she to deprive me of the only time each day—each day except Thursday—when I could be totally alone? Those few precious minutes when I was nobody's brother and nobody's son and nobody's pupil. What an awful thing for her to do, to come between the Winston and the Carmichael.

"What did you learn in school today?" she asked.

I was still annoyed with myself for weakening yesterday afternoon. I wouldn't look up; I didn't want to be disarmed. I could only fire if I didn't see the whites of

37

her eyes. "In school today," I answered, "I learned that flatulence is a polite word for fart."

She laughed. She laughed out loud. "I hadn't expected that," she said. Then she laughed again. "Did you learn anything else?"

I replied, "I also learned that you can get a monstrous hickey from a Kirby vacuum cleaner. Freddie Hauser has one on his neck; he claims it came from a passionate maid." She laughed again. I had fired off two very good shots, and now I dared look up. The battle was over; I won; I surrendered.

"Seventh grade?" she asked.

"Seventh grade," I answered.

"Is it still algebra, history, current events, general science and English?"

"Algebra, history, current events, general science, English and zingers. We try hardest at zingers."

"Will you tell me what *zingers* is?"

"Are. Zingers are put-downs. We practice being sarcastic."

"Can you remember some zingers to tell me?"

"I can remember them all. But I never repeat them."

"Why?"

"Two reasons: one, a true wit never repeats himself; he lets others repeat his remarks for him. And two, if the zingers aren't mine, I'm not going to repeat them and help some other guy's reputation."

She chuckled. Usually only teachers or old aunts chuckle, and usually I hate it. But it was quite a decent sound coming from her. "Yes," she said, "there's another reason, too. Zingers are often untranslatable from their place of origin."

"Did you teach in Ethiopia?"

"I taught for a while."

"Seventh grade?"

"No, English."

"Was that a feeble attempt at a zinger?"

"Yes," she answered. "Actually, I didn't teach English very long. After I went out into the primitive areas, I taught hygiene and health care."

"Did you find it hard to live in a tent after having lived in a nice house like this? I am often told how lucky I am to be privileged?"

"Who tells you?"

"Teachers, clergy and Mother. I often think that I would be very glad to be underprivileged. Is that what you wanted?"

"I don't know if that's what I wanted. I worried a lot about not knowing what I wanted. This is one of the privileges of being privileged. I just knew that I didn't want to be Caroline. After I was kidnapped and then saved, I saw my chance to escape being Caroline. I became Martha Sedgewick."

"Was it difficult to become someone else, to switch identities?"

"In many ways it was easier than I thought."

"For example?"

"At first one of the things I enjoyed doing was excusing Martha. I couldn't be blamed for whatever Martha did. I thought, Caroline didn't do it. Caroline remained cool and perfect. There was, too, the pleasure of allowing my old Caroline self to sit back and watch what my new Martha self was doing. I'd often find myself thinking, 'Go ahead, Martha, prove to Caroline that you can do it.' " She looked at me and said, "There is still a lot of Martha in Caroline. I'm certain that Caroline is a much better person for having been her."

She smiled again, and I recognized what it was about her smile that made it unique. It was unguarded, which was certainly not a Carmichael look. But, then, certainly no one who was not the real Caroline could be that, be unguarded.

I ARRIVED HOME from school on Thursday and found Heidi sitting in the breakfast room just as she always did. But now Caroline sat there, too. Both my sister and my half said, "Hi, Winston," when I walked in, and then they waited. I felt as if they had both entered a contest, and getting my attention was their goal as well as their prize.

I sat at the table, and Caroline got up and walked toward the kitchen saying that she would tell Cora that I was home and hungry.

Heidi watched Caroline leave. "She isn't very nice," she said.

"Oh, I don't know," I answered.

"She hardly talked to me while we were waiting."

"Did you talk to her?"

"The grown-up is supposed to talk first."

"You can't make friends if you make those rules."

At that moment Caroline returned, carrying a plate and a glass of milk. "Your mother went to the beauty parlor," she said.

"We know that," Heidi answered. "Thursday is her day there. Winston and I always play games on Thursdays, don't we, Winston?"

"Yes," I answered. "Yes," I repeated, "we do that."

"That's fine," Caroline said. "I'll be in my room." Then she got up and left.

I followed her with my eyes. I felt bad that she left; I felt bad about the way she left. I looked down at Heidi. "I have a terrific idea for this afternoon," I said. "Let's have a scavenger hunt on the grounds."

I watched Heidi's arms waggle with enthusiasm. "Oh, goody!" she said.

"We'll invite Caroline to hide the things."

Heidi frowned, her face puckering like a dried apple doll. "Not Caroline," she said. "Luellen. Luellen will hide the treasures. We don't need Caroline."

I muttered so that Heidi could not hear, "Maybe. Maybe we don't. Maybe I do."

five

"When did the dinner table first become a proving ground?" I asked.

"Who knows?" she answered.

"I thought maybe you'd remember."

"Can't you?" she asked.

"No. I think it began while I was in a crush of feelings. A whole set of old emotions were washing out, and a new set were chugging in, sloshing around, fitting into corners that had been empty."

She leaned back and smiled as she thought of something. "I don't know when the testing began," she said, "But I certainly remember when it ended."

"At Thanksgiving." I laughed as I thought about that. "Do you remember that first Thanksgiving?" I asked.

"Remember?" she asked. "Could I ever forget?"

"It stands out in my mind, too."

"A Thursday again," she said. "Strange how much of this comic strip takes place on a Thursday."

IT WAS AFTER I was certain about where I stood with Caroline and, more important, where Caroline stood with me that I began to focus on the tests that Mother administered at the dinner table.

I noticed that she would start a test from any direction. "I met Sarah Lamson today," she would begin. Then looking at Caroline, "Do you remember her?"

CAROLINE: No, I'm afraid I don't.

GRACE: Oh, of course. Her name was Sarah Tyrone when you knew her.

CAROLINE (*hesitatingly*): Oh, yes, Sarah . . . Sarah Tyrone, you say?

GRACE (*smiling, an eyebrow raised at Charles*): Sarah.

CAROLINE (*nodding her head, smiling as if to herself*): Silly Sally Tyrone. I hope that Mr. Lamson is smart enough for two; it will take that, you know, for them to have children of only normal intelligence.

I WATCHED Mother's face register a grudging *Pass*.

Another time—it was a Thursday—Mother had been to the beauty parlor. She patted her hair upward and said, "I ran into the most unlikely person in the most unlikely place today."

*   *   *

43

CHARLES: Who would that be?

GRACE (*looking at Caroline*):   Agatha Trollope.

Caroline continued eating and said nothing.

CHARLES: And how was old Miss Trollope?

GRACE: Terribly crippled with arthritis.

Caroline continued eating and said nothing.

CHARLES: Is she retired yet?

GRACE: As a matter of fact, she isn't. She is actively recruiting for Finchley. She asked about Heidi.

At that moment Heidi came to attention; she lifted her head from her hand and demanded, "Who is Miss Trollope?"

GRACE: Caroline will tell you, dear. Caroline knows who Miss Trollope is better than anyone at this table.

CAROLINE (*looking at Heidi*):   Miss Agatha Trollope is the headmistress at Finchley School. You might do well to go to Finchley, Heidi.

HEIDI (*lips pooched out like a kissing gourami*):   But I want to stay at Holton always and always and always.

GRACE (*reaching over and patting Heidi's hand*):   Don't worry about it now, dear.

There were other tests: places and dates, and they were well under way by the time it dawned on me that part of Mother's reasons for inviting Caroline to stay with us was so that she could chart and grade the conversations at our evening meals.

I was slow to notice. I had lost all my desire to be Baby Bear and catch Goldilocks eating forbidden porridge. I had been busy being Columbus, discovering a new world.

By THE END of Caroline's second week, I had begun, timidly at first, and then eagerly, to point my day toward coming home, coming home to Caroline. I could hardly wait to see her in the breakfast room, and except for Thursdays, she was always there. We talked about the world, and we discussed life. We exchanged thoughts and borrowed opinions, but only long enough to consider them and decide if they were good enough to belong to us.

And I had begun a new kind of education. History and geography were no longer subjects; they had become subject matter, subject matter about which I could have conversations with Caroline. I had to know my material to be able to discuss it with her. Being able to talk intelligently about what I had read had become a new kind of accountability, far more difficult than getting A's.

Caroline was the first person I had ever known who had read deeply and seriously out of interest and enthusiasm and not simply to pass a test.

And she was not like certain relatives of mine who gave me books as gifts—books that I knew they had never read themselves, but ones that were GOOD BOOKS, and that they wanted me to associate them with. There were more people who knew what to read than there were people who read. Caroline was not like that. There was a great deal she had not read; she had not read a lot of the GOOD BOOKS. But she had read a lot.

I, myself, had been reading for a long time. I had learned to read even before I had started school. But aside from test-passing and aside from a certain incident in the fifth grade, I had used reading only as a form of entertainment.

IN THE FIFTH grade I had hated my teacher, Mr. Eppes, and I knew that Mr. Eppes hated me. But we kept it polite; such things were kept polite at Wardhill.

I had leafed ahead in my history book and had seen that we were going to study early American history, so I began to read everything I could about Benjamin Franklin. I read with a special kind of fervor; I was reading for revenge. Then I sat back and waited for Mr. Eppes to make a mistake.

He didn't.

We were studying a very patriotic kind of American history; more was left out than was said, so it actually was very difficult for Mr. Eppes to make a mistake. I decided that I had to help out. I raised my hand.

"Yes, Carmichael?"

I cleared my throat. "It is the considered opinion of most scientists that if Mr. Benjamin Franklin really believed that lightning was electricity, he was a fool to go out in a thunderstorm, grounding himself to a kite. He was lucky he wasn't electrocuted."

"That's true," Mr. Eppes replied. "That also happens to be the opinion of some historians as well as some scientists. But historians have the courtesy to add that we, as well as Mr. Franklin, were lucky. It would have been unfortunate for America if Ben Franklin's life had been cut short by a bolt of lightning." He began to turn toward the blackboard, his signal that the discussion was over. I quickly raised my hand, my signal that it was not. "Yes, Carmichael?"

"What is the difference between a *natural* son and a son?" I asked. Mr. Eppes didn't answer immediately. "The reason I'm asking," I went on, "is that Mr. Franklin's son William was a natural son. Does that mean that Mr. Franklin had not married William's mother?" (Of course, I knew the answer; I had looked it up before I asked.)

Mr. Eppes answered very hurriedly, "Yes, it does," and then he turned again toward the blackboard. Before he was a hundred eighty degrees around, I raised my hand again. "Yes, Carmichael?"

"I was wondering, sir, if you could tell me the difference between a *common-law* marriage and a marriage?" Again Mr. Eppes did not answer immediately. I filled in. "The reason I'm asking, sir, is that Mr. Franklin's marriage to Deborah is described as a common-law marriage. Do you suppose that is because she lived with old Ben at the same time she was legally married to some sailor?"

At that point Mr. Eppes said, "Carmichael, I will discuss this matter with you after class."

So he kept me after class, and we didn't discuss Benjamin Franklin at all. We talked about Winston Elliot Carmichael. Mr. Eppes told me that being picky is not being smart. He told me that I ought to begin using my talents to learn and to evaluate information. He told me that he had to admire my strategy—my perseverance was phenomenal.

"Are you going to tell my father about this?" I asked. Father was on the Board of Trustees of Wardhill.

"I am not even going to tell Headmaster Reeves," said Mr. Eppes gallantly.

I asked for permission to leave, and Mr. Eppes granted that. I walked slowly to my next class, thinking that the awful Mr. Eppes had applied the word *talents* to me. Also, he admired something I had done and had referred to something else as phenomenal.

The situation in the fifth grade improved after that day.

MOTHER'S LAST TESTING of Caroline resembled my testing of Mr. Eppes—a frontal attack with cuticle scissors. It occurred on the Monday before Thanksgiving.

MOTHER BEGAN: It has always struck me as the most remarkable coincidence that you should find yourself working at the same nursing home that your Grandmother Adkins was at.

CAROLINE: It was no coincidence at all. I had gone to Grandmother's house as soon as I reached Pittsburgh. I was desperate to see her. I felt that she would tell me what kind of a welcome I would receive from Father.

MOTHER: How did you get in to see her? She had become so impossible—senile and throwing magazines —those last months that no one was allowed . . .

FATHER: Now, Grace. She only threw magazines at that one nurse, the one she called The Enema.

I laughed.

MOTHER: Are you sure she said "Enema"? Wasn't it more likely "The Enemy"? (*Father shook his head no.*) Even so. She was mean and senile. (*then looking at Caroline*) I don't know how you expected to get information, information about Charles's feelings, or anything else for that matter, from her.

CAROLINE: I found that out. Once I learned that Grandmother had to be put in a nursing home, it was not difficult to find out which one. I took the night shift, the only opening they had. By that time, I wanted to help her instead of having her help me. And I wanted some time to sort out my feelings about coming home.

MOTHER: You had had sixteen years to sort those out.

CAROLINE: I was sorting them out *in place*. A person must be far more certain of her actions when she knows they will produce a reaction. I realized that my actions would affect many lives. I had to ask myself what would be the kindest thing to do.

FATHER: Well, I'm certain that you did the kind thing. I'm grateful for your decision to return.

MOTHER: Was your Grandmother Adkins glad you came back?

FATHER (*impatiently*): Oh, Grace! What a question.

Her Grandmother Adkins was in no condition to even know if she was grateful. She didn't even recognize me. On two of my visits she called me Seth.

Caroline kept as silent as a smile, her smile.

THANKSGIVING DINNER at our house was always an evening affair. The turkey dressing varied as did the cook. Cora's was chestnut, and the cranberries were served as a relish. Father always made the first blessing, offering thanks for all the customary things, including the food. Since lack of food was something that I knew about only from movies and books, I thought that Father's offering thanks for it was insincere—like offering thanks for not having acne at his advanced age. Father then asked each of us at the table to say a prayer. Mother was next; she mentioned good health and the safety of her children.

Caroline thanked God for allowing her to enjoy her new life without forgetting her old.

Heidi made the following blessing, holding her folded hands on the table in front of her: "Thank You Lord, for Mummy and Daddy and for Winston, for my teachers, Miss Foyt and Mrs. Schenk, for Sister Clothilde, for Simmons, Luellen and Maurice and for our cleaning lady, Mrs. Wylie, and for Solomon. Thank you also for Cora and all the good food she has cooked for us today." Then Heidi, with her head still bowed, raised her eyes to look at Caroline, sitting by me across the table.

50

I looked at Caroline, too. It was the first time in my life that I had ever heard a prayer that was an insult. I had rehearsed a prayer to myself. I bowed my head, grateful for the privacy that a bowed head allowed, and said, "Thank You, dear Lord, for delivering me out of the depths of ignorance and loneliness and into the company of my beloved sister, Caroline." I kept my head bowed and thought a minute and decided to skip the rest. At last I looked up and through two eye sockets that felt rimmed with orange neon, I read the faces at the table: Mother, annoyed; Heidi, unaware; Father, pleased; Caroline, flattered / embarrassed / quietly, indeed, thankful.

I hoped that my prayer of thanks would stop the testing of Caroline, and it did. But later, when events sorted out, I realized that the time of testing had just passed. The papers, making Caroline the legal heir to the Adkins estate were signed the first Monday in December.

six

"How different the news coverage would be to-day," I said. "Father never even called the television stations then. The evening news allowed all of fifteen minutes to cover Pittsburgh, football, the world."

"Did the news make you a celebrity at Wardhill?" she asked.

"Oh, yes. For a whole day. But for a school where fathers often made front page news, and at least one mother a week was on the society page, that was an accomplishment. Celebrity, like everything else, was more modest in 1952, and I guess that, too, was because of less television." I laughed as I remembered something else. "Barney Krupp mentioned to me that he would like someday to meet my new sister, and I answered, 'You really would, Barney. You really would. She's nothing at all like my other one.'"

She seemed preoccupied. She opened a file folder that was on her desk, she flipped through it, then quickly closed it and placed it in the middle of her desk. She folded her hands over it. She seemed to have to pull herself back to the present. "It was only a short time from then until Christmas," she said.

I nodded.

"Go on," she said. "On to Christmas."

I WAS NOT INVITED to the signing of the papers, and neither was Heidi. Mother said that our being there would be an open invitation.

"Open invitation to what?" I asked.

"Why, to another kidnapping," she said.

The newsmen were there, the network radio stations and the local papers and the news services, AP and UP, as well. The newspaper clippings show Mother and Father standing behind a desk at which Caroline is seated; Caroline is holding a pen. Everyone in the picture is smiling. I learned later that Mother had won a major battle; she had convinced Father that if at any future date, they found conclusive evidence that this woman was not Caroline Adkins Carmichael, the Adkins's fortune would be returned to the Carmichaels. Father had agreed, but he had insisted that it would not be necessary for the woman claiming to be Caroline to return any of the worldly goods she may have received in the meantime. In the picture Caroline is smiling, too. Each of them had a victory to celebrate.

The day following the signing, three hundred engraved invitations were mailed to friends and relatives to attend a reception at our house in Caroline's honor on Christmas Day.

"I would like to take Winston with me to shop for my dress," Caroline announced at the dinner table.

Father looked pleased. Mother did not.

"I thought we could go shopping together," Mother said. "I'd like to take you to the Club for lunch and then we could do the shops." Shopping was Mother's strongest suit. The happiest year in her life had been the year that I grew two sizes in one semester and had to have everything—underwear on out—replaced twice.

"You have enough to do," Caroline said. "Ordering flowers, making arrangements with the caterer. I'll have Maurice drive me to Wardhill, and we'll go to town from there." She looked at Mother and asked innocently, "The stores are still open on Thursday nights before Christmas, aren't they?" I had seen her check the paper to make sure they were.

"Yes, they're open," Mother said. "But can you tell me what the child is to do for dinner?"

"We'll have some supper at Horne's."

Father smiled, "Lunch at Horne's was always a special treat when Caroline was a little girl."

Mother asked Father, "When do you suppose the child will get his homework done?"

"Oh, yes," Father said. "There is that. Well, now, let me see . . ." He looked over at Caroline. She returned his look, almost a look of defiance, and he said to Mother, "Oh! let him go, Grace. The stores close at nine. Even if they stay out until then, I'm sure he can get his homework done when he comes home, if he gets to it immediately."

"Well, I don't know," she said. "I don't like him wandering about town late at night. And what about Heidi. What will Heidi do?"

And then Caroline said something that almost ruined it altogether. She said, "Come now, Grace, don't you think he deserves a Thursday off. You escape every Thursday."

Mother's face grew as gray as a raw oyster. "I don't know what you mean."

"I think you do," Caroline said.

Mother looked at Father and then nodded, a cold, stiff jerk of her head, and said, "See that he's home by nine." She left the room with a cold, stiff walk.

CAROLINE CHOSE QUICKLY—almost without vanity. She modelled the gown for me, a deep purple dress that the saleslady insisted upon calling *aubergine*. While the seamstress was marking the dress for hemming and for a few other alterations, I told her that I needed some money to buy something. She opened her purse and asked, "How much?"

I had no idea.

I knew that I wanted to buy her something, something special, something beautiful and just from me. "Oh," I said, "fifty will do."

"How about ten for starters?" she asked.

Ten did very nicely. I found a beautiful book, a slipcased edition of the *Rubaiyat of Omar Khayyam*. I glanced through some of the poems and decided it would be the perfect thing to give her the day of the party at some moment when we were alone. I paid for it, took it to be gift wrapped and paid for that, too. So unaccustomed was I to having money—to having to use money—that it never occurred to me that I had taken hers to buy her a present.

OUR PACKAGES rode up front with Maurice. After having had the dress fitted, she had purchased other necessaries, and I had gone with her from one department to the next. We never left Horne's.

"I like the dress," I said. "Aubergine."

"Eggplant," she said, laughing. "But at least I got shoes and bag to match. I am coordinated," she said triumphantly.

"Do you suppose a trip to Horne's would do it for Heidi?" I asked.

"What do you mean?"

"Get her coordinated," I said.

That was the first time I had ever indicated to Caroline that I realized that Heidi was damaged, not special.

Caroline asked, "Will you feel less responsible for her if she gets coordinated?"

"I think," I said, "that I'd feel relieved." And then I felt guilty saying something like that. But why? Why was Heidi so guarded that I couldn't talk to a friend about her. And Caroline was supposed to be more than a friend. Why should I feel guilty talking to one (half) sister about another?

Caroline stared out the window. She turned toward me and patted my knee. "If we stretch the bars of the cage very wide—very, very wide indeed—even a cripple can walk through." Then she stared out of the window and said nothing the rest of the way home.

I hadn't wanted our evening to end like that. Crippled.

EVEN THOUGH Caroline wore her aubergine and even though she was coordinated, I knew that Mother looked much prettier standing in the receiving line. Caroline stood between Father and me. Mother and Heidi made a trochee at the end. The guests passed down the line, shaking hands.

There was little kissing; most of the kissing I had seen had been at Italian movies.

There was some testing: You probably don't remember me . . . But it was more a test of the person's importance than of Caroline's talent for identification. She remembered more people than she did not. I had to admit that if Caroline wasn't Caroline, she was pretty good at being what Caroline should be.

I saw a large old lady, hair like an ancient dandelion, and using an aluminum walker, bump her way through the doors of the living room. The woman paused on the threshold. Caroline dropped the hand that she had been shaking and ran across the room. "Miss Trollope!" she called. "Miss Trollope, I had given up hopes that you would be able to make it."

I had never seen this Miss Trollope before. I remembered from the scrapbook that she was the headmistress of Finchley, Caroline's prep school. Caroline seemed overjoyed to see her. I had never seen Caroline overjoyed before. *Friendly* was Caroline's style. *Warm friendly* was her style. *Overjoy* wasn't.

Miss Trollope looked hard at Caroline, her breathing visible and audible. "Come, come, Miss Trollope," Caroline urged, "have a seat on the sofa."

Miss Trollope sat down, her hands resting on the walker, the skirt between her knees draped into a gray satin smile. She stared hard at Caroline and then seemed to make a decision. "I want to ask you something, child." There occurred at that moment a conversational synapse, one of those natural pauses in the rhythm of the room. It was a loud silence, full of nerve endings waiting for a stimulus. It came: Miss Trollope's question, a noisy question, an overwhelming question, that only an old lady, accustomed to command and weary of pain would ask.

"Why," she boomed, "why, child, have we not heard from you for all these years?"

Caroline smiled. "I was in love. And there was the war."

"Did love breed amnesia?"

"No. It bred selfishness."

"Are you married?"

"No."

"Were you?"

"No."

"Where is he?"

"Dead."

And the babel in the room began again.

The party became very gay after Agatha Trollope's entrance. Mother moved from cluster to cluster, answering the same questions with the same answers and being her best, being a hostess. She looked smooth and immaculate. Caroline's aubergine had wrinkled and her hair began to frizz; she looked more picturesque than pretty. Heidi, in her petticoats and her curled and ribboned hair was forgotten and ignored.

I watched Caroline become surrounded first by one group and then another. I watched Father lift Caroline's glass from her hand and replace it with another drink, freshly wrapped in a napkin, and I saw Caroline look over her shoulder at him and smile her thanks. Father never moved farther than one cluster away from his new-found daughter.

Heidi sat on one of the sofas against the wall. Without Mother or Maurice or Luellen running interference for her, she was lost in the crowd, like a beribboned, beruffled mushroom, lost in all the talk that entered her head as verbal fuzz.

I walked toward her, and as soon as I was close enough, she welcomed me with that sad flaying of her arms, her elbows close at her waist. I sat down next to her, and she looked up at me, head tilted, eyes squinting, and mouth open: her creature look, I thought.

Then she smiled, a wet bubble, making a convex lens, magnifying her gums. It was a hesitant smile, as alone on her face as her person was in the room.

Some part of her knows, I thought, and suddenly I couldn't bear it. I took hold of one of her hands and said, "Stay here, Heidi. Don't move. I have something for you. Something special."

I ran to my room and brought her the *Rubaiyat of Omar Khayyam*. She took it from me and managed to get it out of its slip cover and opened. Then her thumb found her mouth and her hand rubbed her ear as she made important contact with the book. I watched her until I saw her leave the room—in every sense but physical.

seven

I walked over to the window. The view from the executive floor. A view so good it could be classified as an experience. I could see the roof of Horne's, and the Allegheny River. She stayed behind her desk, behind a barrier of buzzers and special phone sets. "I've thought about jealousy a lot," I said. "I've concluded that it is sometimes necessary."

"Jealousy is a form of pain," she said. "I guess some pain is necessary."

"In my case," I said, "jealousy was a form of lesser pain."

"Less pain than what?" she asked.

"Less pain than a broken heart."

"How would you show jealousy in a comic strip?" she asked.

"Why, I'd color myself green," I said, laughing.

DURING CHRISTMAS RECESS, breakfast was served whenever anyone wanted it. Three of our cooks had quit exactly a day and a half after Christmas envelopes.

Caroline was sitting at the breakfast table when I came down to breakfast, and she waited while I set Cora in motion. I asked Caroline about some of the people who had come to the party. I mentioned that I had seen an old newspaper cutting where they had interviewed Bunny Waldheim when she had been Bunny Miller. I mentioned that they had also interviewed Agatha Trollope. "Everyone said that Caroline Carmichael was very nice," I concluded.

"Bunny's nice, too," Caroline said. "She's invited me to her house. She is married and has a young family, and still she's gone back to college to get a Ph.D."

Heidi toddled to the table. She climbed onto a chair, her normally bumpy climb made even more so, being off balance from carrying the *Rubaiyat*. The book already looked as if it had gone through a steam bath. She put the book on the table and leaned her head on one hand and put her thumb in her mouth. I began the silent treatment, but Caroline looked at Heidi and asked, "Did you enjoy the *Rubaiyat?*"

Heidi took the thumb out of her mouth and nodded yes and then replaced her thumb.

"Which poem did you like best?" Caroline asked.

Heidi removed her thumb from her mouth, shrugged her shoulders and put her thumb back into her mouth.

"Did you read them all?"

Heidi removed her thumb from her mouth, nodded and put her thumb back into her mouth.

"What were they about?"

Heidi shrugged, thought a minute and said, "About how to be happy."

"I'll bet you didn't even read them," I said.

"I did, too," she said, wiping her thumb on her skirt.

Caroline opened the book and asked Heidi to read to her, and Heidi did. Caroline was more impressed than I thought she ought to be. Caroline leafed through the pages and picked out another verse at random.

"*Some for the Glories of this World . . .*" Heidi read.

"Do you understand the poems?" Caroline asked.

Heidi nodded yes. I saw that Caroline was examining Heidi in a new light; I didn't like what I saw.

"Liar!" I yelled at Heidi. I closed the book on her thumb and demanded, "Tell me what just one of them means."

Heidi rubbed her thumb and looked over at Caroline and then at me. She stuck her thumb back into her mouth and climbed down from the chair and, holding her book under her arm, galumphed away.

"Chimpanzee!" I screamed. Then, trying to sound detached and amused, I said to Caroline, "She's really nothing but a monkey, you know. The words don't mean a blessed thing to her. You could teach a monkey to read the way she does. She recognizes the shapes of words the way an illiterate recognizes the shape of road signs."

Caroline said gently, "I think her ability to read is rather remarkable."

I felt my face grow red as I continued my argument, "You can't really discuss anything with her, you know.

The only thing she ever thinks about is getting her own way."

"Maybe that is all she has ever been given to think about." Caroline added in a gentle voice, "I think her ability to read shows something special. It means that the words are in her. A lot of non-Heidi words." I knew I was blushing, fighting a very private rage of a kind that I remembered from when I was little, from the time when I had first had Heidi to consider. Caroline waited; she watched me choke up; jealousy is hard to swallow. Then she said, "Heidi has two drawbridges to let down before she can leave the castle."

THAT DAY MARKED the entrance of Heidi into the small incandescent world that I had marked off for Caroline and for me alone. Now, for the remainder of the winter holiday, whenever Mother was not at home—and that was often, for the Christmas season was full of parties—Heidi joined Caroline and me. Luellen and Cora were alternating days off, and we often ate dinner in the breakfast room, just the three of us.

One day as the three of us sat at the table in the breakfast room, Heidi picked up a knife and made an effort at buttering a roll. She glanced up at Caroline and waited, and Caroline nodded, and then Heidi smiled that warm, wet, funguslike smile of hers. When I saw Caroline beaming her approval at those pitiful fingers working as if each were wrapped in dryer lint, I felt a small surge of that green rage again.

Several times Heidi tried to interrupt our conversations, but Caroline would not allow that. So Heidi became a quiet listener, more a mascot than a pest. But as soon as Mother returned, Heidi became her old self. Cutsey, clinging and cuddling. Neither Caroline nor I said anything to Mother.

Why?

Why didn't I tell Mother that Heidi was trying out normalcy. Perhaps because I had been taught that I was never to mention Heidi's difference. Perhaps because I wanted to see how far Heidi would go, how far she could go. Perhaps because I felt it was Heidi's right to tell whenever she chose to. Or perhaps, just perhaps, some hidden part of me wanted her to always be the golliwog.

If Caroline had her own reasons for saying nothing to Mother, I never asked what they were. I never discussed it with Caroline. I had been taught a habit of silence.

JUST AS ALL STARS swell and grow especially luminous before they die, so it was with the planet Carmichael. It had swelled to include Heidi, and it had grown brighter as it had grown bigger, but it, too, was about to die. Caroline had chosen an apartment; she would move out with the new year.

eight

One of the buttons on her desk lit up; she threw a switch and her secretary announced over a conference phone speaker that the president of Hooton had called twice. "Oh," she said, "tell him he'll have to wait. We're about to get to Bunny Waldheim." Then she threw the switch again, and all the buttons on her desk went dark. She held her fingers over her mouth for a time, gazing out over her desk. Her eyes at last focused on me. "What color," she asked, "would you color Bunny Waldheim?"

"Easy," I answered. "In the sixties, I would have colored her beatnik; now, in the seventies, I would have to color her hippy. But then, when we first met her, I would have had to color her burgundy for that foyer and blue for her jeans. Burgundy and blue, I guess. And on that first day I would have colored her pink."

"Do you mean McCarthy pink? The famous Fifties pinko?"

"Oh no. Not pink as a shade of Communist red. Baby pink."

"Yes," she said. "I remember. There was that infant."

CAROLINE MOVED OUT the day that school resumed. I came home, hoping that something would have delayed her, hoping that she would still be there, but she wasn't. Her new place was on Fifth Aveune, high up on a bluff overlooking the trolley tracks. She had chosen one of the first big apartment buildings that had replaced an old mansion. That evening she called to give me her new phone number and to invite me to visit whenever I wished. "Say *hello* to Heidi for me," she said before hanging up.

I didn't. Phone calls were something I could have that Heidi couldn't; I'd keep it that way for a while.

The first Thursday after Christmas recess I saw Caroline waiting for me instead of Maurice. She had taken her driving test, and as part of his private celebration at having her (officially) back, Father had given her a car, a small car, a Hudson two door, gunmetal gray. I ran out, my math book slipping and bending the metal spiral of my notebook and causing marks like mice tracks to appear on the palm of my hand. I ran toward the car and stopped short. Heidi was in the front seat.

"Get in back," I said to Heidi.

"Get in back yourself."

"Someone seeing your cretin face up front can cause an accident."

"Yeah? Then how come I don't cause any accidents when I ride up front with Maurice?"

"Because Maurice is the only person in Pittsburgh with a face funnier than yours."

"Then we should have double accidents. Double. Double. Double. Double. Double. Double."

"Heidi," I yelled. "Shut up, or I'm going to stuff my shirt sleeve into your mouth—with my arm in it. Now move over. We'll all three sit up front."

Heidi bumped her way over to the middle of the front seat, and I climbed in beside her. I looked over at her, and I said, "You stink!"

And Heidi answered, "If I stink, I don't know how a snot-nose like you can smell me."

I laughed. I had to hand her that round.

Caroline laughed, too. I know now that the name-calling and the name answering that happened that afternoon represented progress. I did not hide my feelings, and Heidi did not hide behind Mother's skirts. We argued as a brother and a sister should; we argued as equals. I got into the front seat, jabbing Heidi as much as I could with my elbows, and making a huge pretence of adjusting my books. Heidi poked me back, and that, too, was brotherly and sisterly.

"Where are we going?" I asked Caroline.

"To Bunny Waldheim's."

BUNNY WALDHEIM lived on Centre Avenue in a section of town that had no name; it wasn't Schenley or Oakland or Squirrel Hill. Just Centre Avenue, a combination of big old houses and small new apartments. Bunny lived on the first floor of one of the big old houses. The entrance foyer was painted burgundy red and there were three doors leading from it.

Caroline rang the doorbell of the first door to the right, and Bunny Waldheim answered. She was wearing blue jeans and carrying an infant that could only be described as half-naked. Bottom half.

"Hi!" Bunny Waldheim said, "c'mon in." Then she called, "Simon! Rosalie! Come, they're here."

Two little kids, the older one a boy, came out of the back of the house, into the living room. Bunny Waldheim put the baby into a playpen, which was set up in the dining room. (It was a girl, and I looked more than was sophisticated.) Bunny Waldheim leaned down to the playpen and very efficiently diapered the baby. She stood up and said, "Now!" Then she reached out her hand and said, "Hi, Winston. Hi, Heidi."

I wasn't certain that women were supposed to shake hands without washing right after diapering a baby girl. I wasn't certain that women were supposed to shake hands at all; it seemed foreign to me—like an Italian movie. But I shook her hand. Heidi wouldn't. Heidi sucked her thumb and held onto Caroline's skirt at the same time, as if she was receiving current and plugging it in.

"How about some milk and cookies?" Bunny Waldheim asked.

Caroline answered for us and said that would be fine. Bunny Waldheim washed her hands before putting the cookies (Oreos and Nabisco vanilla wafers) on a plate. Also, I was glad to note that the glass that she poured the milk into was not too badly smudged and only on the outside toward the bottom. I needed to use the bathroom, but I didn't feel safe about that yet. I feared that Bunny Waldheim's bathroom might be as bad as Wardhill's just before school let out. It could be worse. It could have tiny curly hairs in the bathtub and embarrassing things showing in the medicine cabinet. And worst of all: wet diapers, smoldering. I thought it best to hold my water, for I wanted very much to like Bunny Waldheim, and I already had had to overlook her naked baby.

Just then the baby in the playpen began to whimper, and Bunny Waldheim gave her a pacifier saying, "Her mother had an exam today, and her baby-sitting arrangements fell through, so I volunteered to help out."

When I heard her say that, I immediately asked if I could please use the bathroom.

I returned, thinking that we, Bunny Waldheim and I, could be very good friends, after all.

Bunny Waldheim asked Heidi if she would like to read a story to Simon. She gave her *The Wind in the Willows*. Heidi took it without a single hint that it was not a particular favorite of hers and sat down on the sofa with Simon on her left and Rosalie on her right and began.

While Heidi read, we three sat at the dining room table and partly listened and partly talked. Bunny Waldheim seemed to listen to Heidi's reading as if she had never heard the story before.

Caroline asked, "Do you see much of our Miss Agatha Trollope?"

Bunny Waldheim answered, "After getting over being furious at her for giving me a high school diploma without teaching me that water does not run uphill simply because I want it to, I called her and admitted that I had had a pretty good education. It had prepared me to be flexible, adaptable. I don't think we can ask for much more than that. She was pleased and asked me what I was doing. I told her. She sometimes calls on me now to test some of her students. I always donate my services, my alumna contribution."

"She still frightens me," Caroline said. "I think . . ." She didn't finish because Bunny Waldheim's head had turned toward the living room, and so then did Caroline's. Heidi had stopped reading.

Heidi appeared in the archway between the living room and the dining room, her thumb marking her place in the book. "Your little girl won't sit still, and she keeps smelling the book."

"All right, Heidi," Bunny Waldheim said, gathering Rosalie to her. "How would you like to draw? Would you like to draw a picture of a man for me?" Bunny Waldheim asked.

"I do ladies better," Heidi said. She sat at the dining room table and grabbing the pencil in her fist as if she were holding a full-sized flagpole, she drew. Drew what? Drew a something that she called a lady. "It never comes on the paper the way it is in my head," she said. Then she tipped her head and pooched out her lips: her precious look.

The precious look was lost on Bunny Waldheim who held up the picture and shook her head and said, "Yeah! that's pretty bad."

Heidi's face fell so fast that I thought I could hear it. Her thumb was into her mouth in an instant, and she came over and stood by my chair. I put my arm around her.

I couldn't remember ever having done that except the time we were having our portrait painted, and the artist had required it.

We went to Bunny Waldheim's the next Thursday, and the Thursday after that, too. One Thursday she played a record, Beethoven it was, and she watched Heidi while the record played. Another time she had a set of special blocks and asked Heidi to arrange them according to a picture she showed her. Heidi did that with little trouble.

When Heidi was in the next room with Simon and Rosalie, Bunny Waldheim asked Caroline, "Can't you bring her earlier? I need a whole day."

"How about a Saturday?" Caroline asked. "I'll arrange with Sister Clothilde, her piano teacher."

"Piano lessons?" Bunny Waldheim asked.

Caroline nodded.

And Bunny Waldheim said, "Poor, poor baby." Then she remembered that I was there. She raised her eyebrows: a question. I nodded: my answer. She knew that I wouldn't tell.

*   *   *

72

CAROLINE MADE UP a story about a party at Bunny Waldheim's, a very small, very exclusive party. Mother only knew of Bunny as Bunny Miller of the Aluminum Millers. Caroline never mentioned Centre Avenue or the burgundy-painted foyer or the half-naked baby, and neither did I.

On the way there, Caroline explained to Heidi that Bunny Waldheim wanted to see her alone and that we would pick her up at three thirty. Heidi's thumb shot straight into her mouth, and she shook her head no. No-no. No-no. No-no. The back of her head rubbed the back of the seat so hard that I expected the upholstery to show a worn spot.

Caroline pulled the car onto a side street and said, "Heidi, look at me. I want to talk to you." Heidi would not look at Caroline, and Caroline lifted Heidi's face by the chin. Heidi closed her eyes. "Winston," Caroline said in exasperation, "please make her listen."

I reached over from the back seat and landed a chop in the crook of Heidi's arm. Her thumb left her mouth with the sound of a stopper being pulled from a drain. She looked back at me, and whatever she had wanted to say wouldn't come. Instead she burst out crying.

"You know Bunny Waldheim isn't going to hurt you," I said. "She just wants to get to know you better."

"I'm not afraid she's going to hurt me," Heidi answered.

"Well, what in the name of Pittsburgh's gray skies are you afraid of?" I asked.

"Nothing," Heidi answered.

"You're not crying like that for nothing," I insisted. "Are you scared of being left without someone from the family?"

Heidi shook her head no.

"Do you want me to call Bunny and cancel?" Caroline asked, gently.

"No," Heidi answered. She stared out the windshield, wiping her nose with her hand, and said, "I'll go through with it."

I said, looking at the back of her hand, "I hope that's not the thumb you suck. You must eat a pint of snot every week," I muttered.

Heidi didn't even respond. She continued looking out front, and Caroline patted her knee, the way she had once patted mine, the day we picked the aubergine. Caroline said, "Brave girl."

Caroline, Heidi and I all knew the real purpose of the visit to Bunny Waldheim's and each of us was fearful of the findings, each to a different degree. Each for a different reason.

We took Simon and Rosalie to the Highland Park Children's Zoo. As we drove north on Negley Avenue, Caroline pointed out a house on the right-hand side of the road, near where Negley ended, and said that it belonged to Miss Trollope.

"Have you visited her since the reception?" I asked.

"No," she answered. "I know I'll have to some day, but . . ."

"Let's go now," I suggested.

Caroline laughed. "If Miss Trollope wants to visit the

zoo, she need only walk out her door. I don't think she'd regard it kindly if we brought the zoo to her." She tilted her head toward the back seat, toward Simon and Rosalie.

"Yeah," I answered. But I sensed something unnatural in Caroline's voice. I filed that sound with Caroline's reaction at the reception.

When we picked up Heidi from Bunny Waldheim's, she seemed in much better spirits than when we had left her there. My spirits were low because I was plain exhausted. Taking Rosalie and Simon to the zoo was not a simple way to spend a Saturday. I think that there was not one square inch of me that had not been tugged at or pulled or poked. And I spent the trip home wishing for a bath and thinking of appropriate deaths for the man who invented cotton candy. I thought he should be rolled in his product and then set on an ant hill.

TWO SATURDAYS LATER—it was February and the weather was gray and wet—I looked up Fifth Avenue as we came out of the library. Pittsburgh looked like it had dissolved into its own products: steel and glass and coal dust. Nowhere was there any color even a quarter note above gray. I needed some sunshine, so I said to Maurice, "We'll go to Caroline's for lunch today instead of Webster Hall."

"But, Winston," Maurice protested.

"It's perfectly all right," I said. "We're invited to drop in anytime."

"I still have to call your home and let them know."

"We'll be home at the usual time. Don't worry about it."

There was a man's umbrella dripping in the hallway just outside Caroline's door. She had company, obviously, but I would not turn back and admit to Maurice that we would have to go to Webster Hall after all. I rang the doorbell. My father answered.

I was surprised. Speechless. I knew that Father had every right to visit Caroline. I reminded myself that she was supposed to be as much his daughter as I was his son. I glanced down at Heidi. She looked as surprised as I did. Of course, it was perfectly logical that Father would visit Caroline at her place: she never came to the house anymore. Still I felt uneasy. Without even entering I felt that I was intruding.

"Come in. Come in," Father said. Then he called toward the kitchen, "Caroline, guess who's here!"

I heard Caroline say, "I'll bet it's Winston."

"Heidi, too," Father added.

"Good," Caroline said, still talking from the kitchen. "Tell them to stay for lunch."

I breathed a little easier when I heard that. Then she came out of the kitchen, smiling. She helped Heidi out of her coat. She said to Father, "Send Maurice home. You'll drive them back, won't you, Dad?"

Dad, I thought. *Dad? Dad!*

While Father went downstairs to dismiss Maurice, Caroline hung Heidi's coat in the closet. I noticed Father's coat there, too. And something else: a golf sweater. I had never seen Father wear a golf sweater around the house except in Palm Beach when we went there for Easter, and that was only once or twice when he was very relaxed. Very.

Lunch was good. Salami sandwiches on rye bread that had seeds in it and a wonderful crust besides. Caroline put some sliced salami on a plate for Heidi, and Heidi cut it up and ate it with a fork. Caroline's eye steered Father's attention to Heidi, and he smiled at her—not the way he smiled at her when Mother did that same thing with the eyes: he smiled at her absent-mindedly. I wasn't sure he realized what Heidi was doing that was different.

We all cleared the dishes from the table after lunch. Heidi did, and Father did, too. Then Father poured two cups of coffee and brought one into the living room and handed it to Caroline. "One sugar and only a dash of cream," he said. Caroline took the cup from him as if it were the most natural thing in the world.

We left after Father finished his cigar. As we drove toward home, I watched Father's back stiffen, and I saw his mouth set into the familiar, neutral looks I had learned to read. The man who had poured the coffee at Caroline's spoke some warmer, foreign, facial language.

nine

The big desk buzzed for her attention again. And again she told whomever it was that he would have to wait. "Where are we now?" she asked, turning back to me.

"Now we're up to Easter."

She looked puzzled.

"What's the matter?" I asked.

"I was just trying to think of how you indicate that time has passed in the comic strips."

"Easy," I said. "There appears a little box in one of the frames and it says, LATER."

"Oh, yes," she said. "That is how it's done. Time passes so easily in the funny papers."

"Easily and painlessly."

I NEVER particularly minded Palm Beach, but I never particularly enjoyed it, either. It just meant that spring vacation had arrived, and here we were.

For Mother, Palm Beach meant doing the same things in different proportions. She still played bridge and shopped, but there was more golf. For Father it meant a long weekend away from the office. He always flew down on the Thursday evening before Good Friday and stayed until the Tuesday morning after Easter. For me it meant a lot of the Invisible Game and a lot of tennis lessons. I never particularly enjoyed either. Heidi and I were the only children around.

For a couple of years Mother had invited Judy. Judy was our cousin, Mother's sister's daughter—Judy Robinson from Muncie, Indiana. She was five years older than I, a pleasant girl in the awkward position of being something between a guest and a servant. Were it not for the generosity of my mother, her Aunt Grace, Judy could not have afforded the luxury of a resort vacation; but were it not for the needs of my mother, her Aunt Grace, she would not have been asked in the first place. Judy was our overseer on the days that Luellen had off.

I liked Judy, but last year I knew she would not be asked back. Last spring Mother had caught her kissing a lifeguard from a public beach while Heidi and I sat on the floor of the same room, playing a game of double solitaire and casually watching cousin Judy.

I seemed to have more time for me this year. It was not just that Judy was gone; there was also less of Heidi. Heidi seemed more self-contained.

I wrote some letters:

Dear Barney,

Have it on the best authority—President Eisenhower's golf score is the same as his IQ. This makes his golf handicap better than his mental one.

> Sincerely,
> Win

Dear Mr. Eppes,

The Seminole Indians of Florida have agreed to sign a peace treaty with the United States if the Secretary of the Interior will offer up a live sacrifice of one social studies teacher per year. I see the negotiations as doomed to failure; of the thousands of social studies teachers in the U.S. only fourteen can be certified as alive. Can you enlist volunteers?

> Sincerely,
> Winston Elliot Carmichael

And then one day something happened which caused me to write:

Dear Caroline,

Florida is fine; lots of people congratulated us on getting you back; they read it in the local papers, so you see, you are still famous. They were sorry

80

that you didn't come to Palm Beach with us. I think they are curious about you. Who wouldn't be?

I am curious, too. Curious about something that happened today at the beach. We were going to have a cookout. Father was going to grill steaks out-of-doors. Mother didn't want us to hear Father's possible language as he tried to start the fire, so she sent us to the beach.

Luellen and I always have to walk Heidi into the water, Luellen takes one hand, and I take the other, and Heidi walks between us like a wishbone. Once she is in the water, she doesn't swim, but she moves easier in the water than she does on land. Here is what happened that was strange: Heidi began to sing. It was not a melody, and if those sounds had come from someone else, you wouldn't call it singing, but knowing her as well as I do, I knew it. I was surprised because I don't remember the last time I heard her singing, but I must have heard it sometime—otherwise how would I have recognized it?

"What are you so happy about?" I asked.

"I am a genius," she answered.

"Yeah," I said, "and your father is Albert Einstein."

She gave a look that I can only describe as a Heidi look, and then she said, "Well, I'm just as smart as you are."

"I'm no genius," I said.

"You're not?" she said. (She sounded really surprised!)

"Who told you that you're as smart as me?"

"Caroline. Bunny Waldheim told her."

Now the reason that I am writing this letter is this: How would Caroline, that's you, have told Heidi that she was as smart as I was unless you were seeing Heidi secretly? And here's another reason I'm writing this letter. Why, if you are seeing Heidi secretly, why didn't you tell me? And here's my third reason—I have always thought, ever since you came back, that you were my friend. I never thought a friend does things like talk to a friend's sister without telling the friend.

I hope you had a nice Easter. We had ham.

Sincerely,
Winston

Caroline's answer, except for her signature was typed.

Dear Winston,

May I please have your trust, your confidence and your silence awhile longer?

Please,
Caroline

I gave her my silence.

82

CAROLINE CALLED almost as soon as we returned home. She told me that she would like to pick me up from school on Thursday.

"Check with me on Wednesday night," I said. "That is, if your finger isn't too sore from dialing this time."

"Winston," she said, "I have some important things to tell you. Will you be there on Thursday?"

"I've just checked my five-day horoscope. It said Thursday was the day for me to avoid encounters with strangers. Are you strange?" I asked.

"When you hear what I have to say, you might even call me weird," she said.

"Oh, good," I said. "Then I'll be there. My horoscope recommends weird."

I WAS QUIET in the car. I wanted to punish her. When we arrived at her apartment, I noticed a cigar butt in an ashtray—Father's. I was quiet about that, too. She opened the refrigerator and took from it a whole Joyce's cream pie. I never knew that you could buy them that way, whole. "How about that?" she said.

"Yeah," I said. "How about it."

I knew it was a peace offering. She cut me a large slice, and I took a huge mouthful. "Well," I said, "this sure beats the camel snot they served at school today. They called it tapioca."

"Winston," she said, "I want to tell you something. I'm going back to college."

I swallowed hard. "But why? You've just moved in.

You don't even have all the furniture you need for this place yet. You don't even . . ."

"Oh! I'm not moving. I'm going to the University of Pittsburgh. I'll just commute up and down Fifth Avenue."

"Good!" I said, relieved. I began to relax. I didn't really want to stay mad at her. I didn't really. "What are you going to study?"

"I plan on enrolling in the special education program."

"Is that because you're so old?"

"What has my age to do with anything?"

"I just wondered if you would need a special education because of your age."

"My age has nothing to do with anything. The course I want to study is called special education. I want to learn how to teach the handicapped."

"Is Bunny Waldheim the one who got you interested? Being that she is going back to college and all."

"No," she answered. "Heidi is the one who got me interested."

"Heidi?" I said. "Heidi? Heidi. It's always Heidi. Everything is for Heidi. I think God made the skies for Heidi, and I think that Andrew Carnegie made Pittsburgh for Heidi, and I think that Eisenhower went to Korea to make the world safe for Heidi." I looked at her and asked, "Why?" I asked softly at first, "Why?" and then I screamed. "Why? Why does Heidi deserve everything? Why does Heidi deserve you?" Caroline reached across the table to me, and I jerked back. She got up

84

and stood behind my chair and put her arms around me. I did not realize that I was being embraced. My first reaction was to pull away from her touch, her very warm, very human touch, but she kept her arms around me, and I relaxed. I didn't cry because I couldn't; knowing how to cry had been taught out of me.

Caroline sat down again. She reached for my hand across the table and waited until we were face-to-face before she said, "Heidi is really my second order of business, Winston." She paused before she added, "You are my first." I pulled my hand back. She lit a cigarette. "Remember months ago, the day we bought the aubergine, I said that if we stretch the bars of a cage very wide, even Heidi can walk through. I thought then that if we stretched the bars just a little, you could walk through and then we would stretch them just a little more, and Heidi could walk through. But I had it backwards, Winston. I realize now that Heidi must go first. You are strangely tied to her. If I can do something to help make Heidi into a whole human being, Winston, you will no longer be responsible for her. You can stop feeling guilty for being handsome and whole.

"Bunny Waldheim has determined—you knew, didn't you, that she was testing Heidi that Saturday we went to the zoo?"

I nodded.

"You knew, and so did Heidi. Bunny did some tests at Holton Progressive, too. I went with her that day, and by the way, there is your answer to how Heidi found out that she has above-normal intelligence. As a matter of fact, Heidi is extremely bright. Bunny feels, and I do, too, that the way out for Heidi is by building up her positives, especially her intelligence. The answer certainly does not lie in disguising her handicaps with ribbons and ruffles and every kind of indulgence. None of the solutions is pretty. Her hearing can be helped with a massive hearing aid, not a pretty one, and her coordination can be helped with braces and with some relearning, a long process, a difficult one, too. That's what I want to learn how to do: diagnose and prescribe for people like Heidi."

"How long will it take you to graduate?" I asked. "How long before you can help Heidi out?"

"It will be some years." She smiled at me.

"Why can't you just hire some people to help her now?"

"You suddenly seem anxious. I must make some other people anxious. Before I can make them anxious, I'll have to make them understand. I have to educate them."

"Tell me," I asked. I didn't want to ask, but I had to know. "Is Heidi smarter than I am?"

"I don't have the figures on you, boy, but I think one of you is as smart as the other." Then she leaned clear across the table and her hands on either side of my head and kissed my forehead. I felt dumb. Like a Norman Rockwell cover for the *Saturday Evening Post*.

AFTER CAROLINE dropped me at home, I went immediately to my room. There sitting on the floor by the doorway, her back resting against the door jamb, was Heidi. "How was Caroline?" she asked.

86

"Fine," I answered as I stepped over her and walked into my room.

She got up and followed me in. "I know you were there. There's no point in denying it."

"I'm not denying it."

"I hope you had a rotten time," she said.

"Well, it so happens that I didn't. She had a whole cream pie."

"Then I hope you have a rotten time the next time you go."

"I don't know if I can stand any more of your good wishes. Better save the rest for Christmas."

"Next week I won't be going with you to Caroline's either."

"That's fine," I said. "Fine with me. More pie."

"I won't be going there ever again. Ever."

"Why not?" I asked. I was surprised.

"Mummy explained it all. Mummy said that I'm getting to be too big a girl now. She says that probably I'll have to start going with her to Mr. Rick's to have my hair done. I'll probably start going to Mr. Rick's very, very soon."

"Do you really want to go to Mr. Rick's instead of Caroline's?" I asked.

"It's what girls do," she said. "You wouldn't understand."

"Caroline doesn't go to Mr. Rick's."

"Mummy mentioned that. She doesn't want me to grow up like Caroline."

"There's no chance of that," I said.

"What do you mean?"

I said, "Nothing." But I thought that there were a lot of ways I meant that. Heidi could never grow up like Caroline. Heidi was made of different stuff; Heidi was made of Carmichael stuff, and Caroline was . . . was what? Caroline was supposed to be Carmichael stuff, too. But I wondered.

ten

"Now, you'll have to tell the plot of the movie," she said. "Do you still remember it?"

"Even after more than twenty years, I can recall it scene by scene. It was in a sense the end of the lies." I thought awhile.

She tapped a pencil on that manilla folder. She was thinking, too.

"You have the right to remain silent," I muttered.

"What do you mean?"

"When they give prisoners their rights, they say, 'You have the right to remain silent.' I think I abused that right. Silence has been called the disease of my generation. I guess it is. What cowards we were." I sighed and said, "We were all cowards except you."

"And her," she added.

HEIDI AND I had a whole Saturday with nothing to do.

Piano lessons did not resume until the second week after Easter. I wondered what Sister Clothilde's Easter had been like. A Convent of the Sacred Heart Easter was probably as different from a Palm Beach Easter as 1953 was different from 1593. I read in the Pittsburgh Press that *Forbidden Games* would be showing at the Squirrel Hill Theater. It was a French movie with subtitles. There was no kind of movie that Heidi enjoyed more. Foreign movies with voices dubbed in were a total loss to her, but those with subtitles made her the equal of everyone else in the audience. Mother called the theater and found out that it was the story of a boy and girl in the French countryside, and she thought that it would be a sweet picture for us to see.

Forbidden Games was indeed the story of a little boy named Michel and a little girl named Paulette. Her mother and father have just been killed in the war. Michel finds Paulette wandering in the countryside. That's about as much of the countryside as the movie has. When he finds her, Paulette is holding her dead dog. Michel feels sorry for her, and he takes her to his farm. He makes a little grave for her dog, and seeing what comfort that gives her, they begin to bury other things like a mole and other small dead animals they find. They make a small cemetery in an abandoned mill. One day they steal the cross from the grave of Michel's brother. When his family discovers the theft, they get very upset. Michel says he will lead them to the stolen tombstone if they promise they will not send Paulette away. When they see the small cemetery, they think that the children have been worshipping the dead. Despite their promise, they send Paulette away. The last scene shows the little girl in the railroad station, not understanding what has happened, and hunting for her friend Michel.

Well, Heidi began to cry when they buried the dog. She warmed up with little sighs while Michel and Paulette were making their cemetery. By the time Paulette is waiting in the railroad station, Heidi had begun real shoulder-shaking sobs and shudders. Something about that poor, bruised, lonely little Paulette reached Heidi and made her ache. She wept like a pitcher of iced tea in July, and when the lights went on, I saw that she was a sight.

I didn't want us to leave our seats until the theater emptied. Luellen, who knew that she would be mistaken for our mother, agreed. We started out as soon as everyone else had left.

What we hadn't counted on was the line of people waiting to get into the next show. Luellen and I walked out with Heidi, red-eyed and sobbing between us. To add to the vision, my sister was sucking her thumb. I couldn't stand it. I pulled her thumb from her mouth and didn't realize until I saw the look of the lady across the velvet rope how cruel I must have seemed. I only hoped that Maurice would be waiting at the curb so that I could immediately dissolve into a dark back seat with my wet lump of a sister.

Mother took one look at Heidi and demanded to

know what had happened. Luellen explained that it had been a very sad movie.

"What is really the matter, Heidi?" Mother asked. Her voice was shrill. "What is it?" she asked again, tipping Heidi's head upward. "Tell Mother what is bothering you."

Heidi shook her head and said nothing. She edged over toward me and took my hand. When she wiped her eyes it was with the hand that held mine, and my palm became moist with her tears. She would say nothing. Mother said, "I know! It's that Caroline again!" Then she threw up her hands and left.

I looked at my sister and said, "Haven't I always stuck by you?"

She nodded.

"You know," I said, "how hard it is for you to stop sucking your thumb?" She nodded. "Well," I said, "you're my bad habit. Don't worry. I won't give you up. I won't let them lie to me."

eleven

"Do you still have the envelope?" she asked.

"Right here," I answered. I took it from the inside pocket of my jacket. "I often think when I watch the Academy Awards Show on television, when the announcer says, 'May I have the envelope, please?' that I already have the envelope, please."

"But you don't have to open it to know who the winner is."

"Correction. I know who the winners are."

THE NEXT THURSDAY I waited until we were at her apartment before I asked, "Why can't Heidi come with us any more?"

"Simple!" she answered. "I have been forbidden to bring her." She gave me a smile that looked like a substitute for tears.

"Who forbade you?"

"Father."

"Why?"

"Because he is a coward!"

How could she call Father a coward? How could she of all people? Father who brings her coffee with one sugar and a dash of cream and Father who smokes a cigar and wears a golfing sweater with her—how could she call him a coward? "What right have you to say such a thing?"

"As much right as you have."

"You do not!" I said. "I am his son, and I would never call him a coward."

"Well, I am his daughter, and I would."

"You are not. You should not."

There was a deep quiet. She pulled in her breath and said, "Is that the way it is with you, Winston? Is that the way? You don't believe that I am Father's daughter?"

"It's not that . . . It's just that you don't seem like . . ." Then I couldn't finish that thought, so I said, "If you were really his child, you wouldn't call him a coward."

"Maybe not," she said. "Maybe if I really were his child, I would not call a handicapped sister, *handicapped*. I would call her Heidi instead of Hilary, and I would make believe that she is cute." She stood up and walked into the kitchen. I followed. From the back of a kitchen cabinet, from behind an electric Sunbeam coffee percolator, she took out an envelope. We walked back into the living room, and she plopped down on the sofa. "I'm tired," she said. "Exhausted." She held the envelope between her thumb and index finger. "I'm tired of all the pretense. Yours and your mother's and your father's. Mine, too." She held the envelope out toward me. "In this envelope is the evidence that establishes beyond a doubt whether I am Caroline Adkins Carmichael or whether I am not. I want to give you this envelope, Winston. I want you to take it home with you. You do whatever you like with it: open it, burn it, use it as a bookmark. You decide whether it is more important to know for sure who I am or whether it is enough to know what I am."

I took the envelope.

"I'll take you home now," she said.

We said nothing to each other all the way home. The envelope rested on my lap, heavy as fate.

I CAME IN through the breakfast room. It was still early. Heidi was sitting at the table—early day at Holton Progressive. I sat down across the table from her. How many Thursdays had it been since we had sat like that? She seemed to catch the mood. "What'll we do today, Winston?" she asked. And she smiled because she really didn't expect an answer. Then she saw the envelope. "Did Caroline give you Joyce's cream pie?"

"Not today."

"Did Caroline give you that yellow envelope?"

"Yes."

"What's in it?"

"A proper case of identification, my dear girl." I

lifted it up toward the light. "Within this plain yellow wrapping is sealed the answer to . . ."

Heidi reached up and grabbed the envelope from my hand. She pinned it under her fist on the table. "Don't open it, Winston. Don't open it. Rip it up. Hide it. But whatever, whatever, whatever you do, don't open it."

"What's the matter?" I asked. I studied her face. She was scared. My sister, the golliwog, was frightened. I had never seen her like that. So alone, so frightened. A kind of fright all the more terrible because she was now fully aware of her isolation. "Why are you frightened, Heidi?" I asked.

"I don't want to know what is in the envelope."

"Aren't you tired of being lied to? Don't you want to know?"

"Yes. I am tired of being lied to. And no, I don't want to know. That envelope doesn't have the lies that hurt. Whatever that envelope says doesn't matter." She looked down at her fist, set heavily like a paperweight on the envelope. "You said, remember, that you wouldn't abandon me?"

"I won't."

"Will you do something brave for me?"

"What? What do you want me to do?"

"I want you to kidnap me."

"That's ridiculous. How can I kidnap you?"

"In a taxi. Just like Caroline."

"Yeah," I said, "to where?"

She looked up at me as if she couldn't possibly understand my innocence. "Why, to Caroline's, of course."

And then I knew what I had suspected that day of the Christmas reception and the days following when Heidi struggled with a fork and the days after that when she had gone to Bunny Waldheim's knowing that she was being measured. I knew something about my sister Heidi—Hilary. I knew that she had all the makings of a brave soul. She had the makings but not the focus. And I knew that I had to answer her bravery with some of my own. I would kidnap her. In a taxi. To Caroline's.

"Your first executive decision," I said.

She laughed. "I guess it was. I've made many others involving a hundred thousand times more money, but there was never one more important. I can close my eyes now and see the look on the cab driver's face when you told him you would sign for the taxi fare."

"He held you hostage in the cab while I ran up and got Caroline."

She laughed. "You see it really was a kidnapping. Caroline paid the ransom."

"Twelve dollars and sixty cents cab fare."

"You weren't worth much more than that then." She put on an old Heidi pout, and I said, "Well, maybe thirteen dollars even."

WE WENT UP to Caroline's and she gave us rye bread and butter while she called Bunny Waldheim and asked her to hurry over.

"What are you trying to do?" Bunny Waldheim asked.

Heidi answered. "Be normal."

Caroline looked at Heidi and said, "You'll never be that Heidi. If I have given you hopes for that, then forgive me."

Bunny Waldheim bent down toward Heidi and tried to soften what Caroline said, "What Caroline means . . ."

Caroline wouldn't let her finish. "What Caroline means is just what she said. What Caroline means is that if Heidi wants to 'be normal' she can just go on home and continue the pretending. If Heidi wants to develop what she has—a fine mind—and if Heidi wants to work—and I mean really work at overcoming her disabilities . . . then I'll agree to call her father and argue her case."

It seemed to me that Caroline could have been kinder. I put my arm around Heidi's shoulder and attacked, "Why did you say 'her father'?" I asked. "Why didn't you say 'my father'? Or 'our father'?"

Caroline's look was cold and tired. "You have the envelope," she said. "You have your answer. Which truth do you want to live with?"

twelve

"I'VE LIVED with truth in a sealed envelope for almost two dozen years," I said.

"How often have you been tempted to open it?" she asked.

"In my days of rage and during my adolescence, at least once a week. Whenever I got angry, I would want to open it. Anger at you. Anger at her. Anything could prompt me to want to open the envelope. And anything could stop me."

"I think I know what really stopped you."

"What?"

"Learning to live with a more important truth."

I shook the envelope, it was now ochred with age, the paper was almost powdery. "What do you suppose is in here? A confession? Do you suppose Caroline made a confession and sealed it in here?"

"The envelope's not thick enough for that," she said. She walked around to the front of her desk. Her walk was smooth and heel-toe, only a brother could recognize some vestige of the galumphing golliwog. And this brother chose not to—knowing the price in pain and practice that she had paid in learning to walk.

"I think today is the day to open it," she said. "You may not know what is in here, but you do know, don't you, what it will tell us?"

I nodded. "How long have you known?" I asked.

"A long time. I've been certain since Father died." She picked up the manilla folder from her desk. "How long have you known?"

"I think I started knowing when I saw Father's cigar butts in her apartment. I had begun suspecting that Saturday we visited her unexpectedly and found Father there. But I didn't recognize what it was until much later. I was in college, enjoying the leisure of a life of literature—a life she gave me, really—when I realized that she loved him. I realized then that by being our sister she had sacrificed ever being his wife."

"Do you suppose Father knew?"

"Some part of Father knew. But Father had grown calluses over all the important nerve endings. He recognized that he felt different—happier—with Caroline than he did with anyone else. But he would never have allowed himself to call it the kind of love that it was. He went along with the myth that she was our sister because he was always uncomfortable with strong emotion, and it suited him better to think that the love he felt for Caroline was the love a father feels for a daughter. I'll bet, though, that he spent many a sleepless night worrying about how he felt about Caroline."

One of the buttons on her desk lit up. She reached across and answered, "Hilary Carmichael here." She listened and said, "I'll see him tomorrow." She pushed the button to off and held the famous old envelope to the light. Then she turned to me and smiled, "How many times have you done that?"

"Over the course of the past twenty-three years? I'd say about a thousand—about once a week—taking time off for a doctoral thesis and a honeymoon."

"Open it today," she urged. "Today will be a good day to do it."

She handed me the envelope. I took an enamel-handled letter opener from her desk. The paper was so old that there was almost no tearing sound. Two pieces of paper fell out. They had been wrapped in a blank sheet of stationery from Finchley School.

One was the academic record of Caroline Adkins Carmichael at Finchley School. There were some D's, but mostly C's. Math had been dropped in her junior year and her senior year, too. The other was the record of the school testing program. On the individualized Wechsler-Bellevue Intelligence Test, Caroline had scored 92. On the Stanford Binet, 97.

Heidi and I smiled at each other. Of course. The Caroline who came back had to be far more intelligent than the real one. She had to be smart enough to be two people.

"I think now that you are ready for this," Heidi said. She walked around to the presidential side of her desk and handed me the manilla file folder she had been fingering all morning.

"Here's some of the best reading you'll do since the *Rubiyiat of Omar Khayyam*," she said.

CONFIDENTIAL REPORT ON MARTHA SEDGEWICK

Submitted by Miss Agatha Trollope,
Headmistress, Finchley School

IT WAS WHILE the Carmichael family was in Palm Beach in the spring of 1953 that the woman calling herself Caroline Carmichael made her first visit to me. I was not surprised to see her. I knew that she would appear sooner or later.

She came to the point of her visit quickly. "Miss Trollope," she said, "I've decided to return to college. I would like to get a bachelor degree, so I shall not be returning to the junior college I attended before . . . before . . . my disappearance. There will be no need for me to transfer any of my credits from there, but the University does insist upon having my high school record. That's why I'm here. I was wondering, Miss Trollope, if you still kept copies of records from, say, as long ago as when I graduated."

I smiled as I began to suspect what was on the lady's

mind. "And, may I ask, is the University requiring you to take some entrance exams? Are they subjecting you to a testing program?"

"Yes, as a matter of fact, they are."

I knew now what the woman wanted. I was half-willing to comply. I liked her well enough, but I wanted to know more. "Why do you choose to return to college?" I asked.

"I have a project. I want to get a degree in special education. I want to teach the handicapped."

"All the handicapped?"

"A single person hardly can be expected to teach all the handicapped," she said.

"A single person can expect to teach a single handicapped person."

"Yes," she answered. "Yes, she can."

"A noble notion," I said. I studied her a long time.

At last I said, "The resemblance is remarkable, but," I added softly, "you are a much nicer person."

She seemed to breathe a sigh of relief. "Thank you," she said. "If Caroline Adkins Carmichel had had the opportunities I have had, perhaps she would be as nice as you think I am."

"Perhaps," I answered, "but, of course, she could never be as intelligent." Then, "You really must love that little girl. What is her name?"

"Heidi. Her real name is Hilary, but her mother calls her Heidi because it is what she wants her to be—something sweet from a storybook. But it is not for her as much as it is for the boy, Winston. He needs to have Heidi freed so that he can be."

"They are lucky children to have an intelligent woman like you helping them."

She laughed. "Yes," she said, "if I were as stupid as Caroline Carmichael, I would never be able to pass the entrance exams for the University. I would have to go back to some place like Candlewood, someplace where one only needs a good family name."

"I won't forge incorrect records," I told her.

She gasped.

I laughed. "But I will agree to say that they have been lost."

"What will you do with the old records?" she asked.

I got up and made my way into the dining room. From the china closet I removed a yellow envelope. "I'm going to give those to you."

"You've been expecting me, I see."

"I've had these records out since the day of that fancy reception. I first suspected then."

Martha smiled. She took the envelope from me. "Thank you," she said.

"Have the University call me. I'll tell them whatever they need to know."

Thus I began my long acquaintance with Martha Sedgewick. From subsequent visits I learned the following facts of her life as they apply to her masquerading as Caroline Adkins Carmichael. I set down these facts, not in the order I learned them, but in the order they happened.

In 1952 Martha Sedgewick returned to the United States from Ethiopia where she had lived for sixteen years. She had gone to Ethiopia with her mother and father who were teachers. She returned an orphan. She did not return to her native Chicago, but went instead to Pittsburgh to find the sister of Harris, the man she had loved and worked with in Ethiopia. Harris's sister was dead. He had no other living relatives, and neither did she. She was depressed. She didn't want to adjust to Eastern Standard Time, and she didn't want to face Eastern Standard people. So she accepted night duty— 11:30 P.M. to 7:30 A.M.—at the nursing home in Sewickley, Pennsylvania, outside Pittsburgh.

One evening after she had been working at the home for two weeks, she answered a call light from room 12A. She checked her charts to see who it was: a new patient, Flora Adkins, admitted just that afternoon. Martha opened the door and saw an old lady leaning on one elbow, who commenced to stare at her. The old lady stared at her a long time before she held up a forefinger —warped like a bonsai—and said, "Come here, Caroline."

Even in the short time she had worked there, Martha had grown accustomed to answering to strange names. The week before she had been Sylvia (a daughter) to Mrs. Lancaster, the broken hip in 14A, and just two days ago she had been Harris (a former butler!), to Mrs. Stillitoe, arteriosclerosis in 15C. And now she would be Caroline to Flora Adkins, arthritis in 12A. She didn't mind. She would answer to whatever name they chose.

She walked over to the old lady and asked her gently where she hurt. Flora Adkins answered, "In my proud soul. I need a bed pan." Martha laughed. Here was one with a sense of humor. She brought the bed pan and then Flora Adkins said, "I always knew that you would return to help me in my hour of need."

"Yes," Martha replied. "I will be just a few steps away when you need me."

"I knew you would be, Caroline," Flora Adkins answered.

Martha smiled to herself, shrugged and returned to her station.

Flora Adkins called Martha once again that night. She couldn't sleep; she wanted to talk. Martha felt a jot of annoyance. After all, she had taken the night shift because it was almost free of interruptions. "We won't tell Charles that you're back," Flora Adkins said. "Not yet anyway."

"Charles?"

"Your father," Flora Adkins replied.

Martha patted the old lady's hand, ready to go out the door again and said, "Yes, Flora."

"Grandmother!" Flora Adkins insisted. "It is not that I object to the modern practice of having children call their elders by their first names, but I must insist that you call me Grandmother. After all, I've waited a long, long time to hear it."

So Martha leaned down and kissed the old lady's forehead and said, "Good night, Grandmother."

"Now, don't tell Charles."

"Don't worry," Martha whispered. "I'll never see him. No one ever visits when I'm on duty."

Martha returned to her desk again, and this time she pulled Flora Adkins's chart from the file. The patient in 12A had been cared for in her own residence until being admitted to the home. Her mind had become increasingly confused; moreover, she had become hostile to the point of open aggression toward one of her nurses. It had become impossible to find people willing to attend to her. She had been deemed mentally incompetent, and Mr. Charles Carmichael became her legal guardian; it was he who had committed her to the home.

Now, don't tell Charles the old lady had said. Charles Carmichael, Caroline's father, must be the Charles she meant.

Martha soon found out more about Charles and even more about Caroline. Flora rang for Martha every night. "Caroline," she would begin, "do you remember the time . . ."

And it was from those many small beginnings that Martha Sedgewick began to learn about Caroline Carmichael. The old lady had an appetite for detail. Distant detail. The sharpness with which she recalled the past made it hard to remember that Flora Adkins had been declared out of her wits. Of course, the present easily slipped from old people. (Flora sometimes did not remember what she had eaten for dinner.) The past where everything was known and finished and required no action was much more comfortable. Especially at night when the present was dark and threatening. Martha began to look forward to her visits with her patient in 12A. Flora Adkins's *Tales of Caroline* proved to be better company than her own lonely thoughts.

One night—as if some hand other than her own did it—Martha removed her identification badge as soon as the call light from 12A flashed on. She removed it the next night and the next. On the fourth night that she appeared without the tag that declared that she was M. SEDGEWICK, Flora Adkins asked for her pocketbook.

The old lady tried to open it herself, then looked down at her fingers and said, "My hands look like they have been assembled out of miscellaneous parts by a mad plumber."

Martha opened the purse for her and handed her the wallet. She knew that was what Flora wanted. The old lady handed it back to her and said, "Look at the pictures, Caroline. Start with the first one."

Martha began looking through them, and Flora Adkins watched her with a look as intense as her look had been that first evening when Martha had answered the call from 12A. She watched as Martha turned over one picture and then another. Martha took her time; to flip through them quickly would be insulting. She saw a photograph of a bride and a groom, of a distinguished older gentleman, and then she stopped short. She gasped. There smiling at her was someone who might have been herself, a teen-age self, wearing a dress she had never owned, could never have afforded to own. Flora Adkins threw her head back and laughed; her gnarled hands bounced up and down on the bedcovers. She fastened Martha with a stare and said, "You are as lovely as you ever were, Caroline."

Martha continued to hold the picture, saying nothing. Flora Adkins waited and then said, "This is the picture that was in all the papers, Caroline. Your kidnap picture."

Martha Sedgewick's taking off her badge was her first unconscious step into the life of Caroline Carmichael. Her study of that photograph was her second. Her third step was deliberate and was longer in coming, long enough for her to learn from Flora Adkins everything there was to know about the life of Caroline Carmichael. She learned names and relationships, the ground plan of the Carmichael family estate, and as Flora Adkins reminisced evening after evening, she came to recognize faces from the photographs that Flora brought out of drawers and closets, patches of a past she refused to give up.

As the pattern of family and fortune emerged, Martha learned that when Flora's daughter, Anne, had married Charles Carmichael, their marriage had been of as much interest to the financial pages of the paper as it had been to the social. The Adkins family holdings were smaller and quieter than the famous Carmichael millions, but they were considerable. At the time of her marriage, Anne's father had settled half of his estate upon her. Through wise investment and interest, her inheritance had grown into a fortune that could easily have been halved again to make two more independent fortunes. Anne Adkins had left her estate to her daughter, Caroline. Unless Caroline returned to make a claim before her thirty-fifth birthday, the Adkins money would meld with the Carmichaels'.

Flora Adkins did not want that to happen. She did

not resent Charles Carmichael, but she hated his new wife, Grace. She detested her with eighty-two years worth of experience in family relations. There were two children from this second marriage, but Flora Adkins knew almost nothing about them. She had refused to set foot on the Carmichael estate since Grace had come into residence. She obviously did not care if Charles came into the Adkins money, her daughter's money, but she knew that when Charles was gone—he was considerably older than Grace—the Adkins money would pass through him to Grace.

Late that summer, the summer of 1952, the old lady began to sink noticeably. The Caroline lessons covered less new material; they became instead longitudinal reviews of time and latitudinal reviews of ancestry. One night while reminiscing about Caroline's eighth birthday, Flora abruptly stopped speaking. She studied Martha a while before she finally said, "When it appears in the papers, Caroline, I don't want my death attributed to heart failure or cerebral something-or-other. I want them to say, 'cause of death: old age.' Now, that has a ring of dignity to it."

Martha recognized that the old lady was letting her know that she would not live much longer. She requested a replacement for her regular night duties and kept vigil at the bedside of her friend/patient, Flora Adkins, mother of Anne Adkins Carmichael, grandmother of Caroline. Only two nights later she was holding the old lady's hand, not at the wrist to take a pulse, not as a nurse, but holding her hand like a grand-

111

daughter when Flora Adkins opened her eyes, fixed them on her and with the last tiny bit of amperage she had left to her, said, "Go to it, Martha girl!"

Then Flora Adkins died.

Martha folded the lady's hands across her chest and knew that with her dying words, Flora Adkins had commissioned her, Martha Sedgewick, to be an impostor.

But it was Charles Carmichael who was the final factor in her decision.

Martha went to Flora Adkins's funeral. She sat in the back of the small chapel that was in the nursing home. She had arrived late. Charles was the only outsider, the only person besides the residents and the staff of the nursing home to attend. Martha watched him leave; he looked lonely. Perhaps it was only his dark suit amidst all the nursing home gray—green gray walls, gray-haired residents, tattletale gray nurses' uniforms, a sea of gray cable-stitched sweaters—but walking up the aisle from the front of the chapel, the rich Mr. Charles Carmichael looked hurt and lonely and vulnerable. Martha decided at that moment that she would return his daughter Caroline to him.

Her first step toward doing so was to slide into the corner of the pew away from the center aisle. She would hide in the shadows until the time seemed right.

It was Flora's lack of knowledge of the two children that made Martha realize that the deception would be easier than she had thought. She, as Caroline, would not be expected to know anything about the Carmichaels' last sixteen years. Besides, she realized, she would not have to be something other than Martha for all those years in between. She had only to say that Caroline Carmichael had assumed the identity of Martha Sedgewick and had gone off to Ethiopia. There was not even a need to destroy Martha Sedgewick's records. The only small piece of invention that was necessary was the part of the story covering the time when Caroline Carmichael supposedly escaped and assumed the identity of Martha Sedgewick.

That, too, proved surprisingly easy. She, Martha, had been ill during the time that the real Caroline had been kidnapped. So she made up the following tale to tell the lawyers: Martha Sedgewick had died, and Caroline, in cahoots with one of her kidnappers, assumed all of Martha's credentials and went to Ethiopia. It was not even necessary to forge a death certificate for Martha Sedgewick; she maintained that Caroline Carmichael had destroyed it.

Martha's true experiences in Ethiopia could stand for Caroline's, except that she had to be careful never to mention her parents.

Once she had successfully pulled off the deception, she began to enjoy being Caroline. She came to believe that a second identity was a positive step toward good mental health. Except for one thing: The more effective she was as Caroline, the less likely it was that Charles Carmichael could love her as something other than a daughter. But life always provided some compensation. And she had found Winston. Since there was no chance to be his stepmother, she would be his sister, and be very good at that. And that would be easy. She had come to love him.

So it was her love for Winston and her increased recognition of and, eventually, love for Heidi that kept her bound to the role of Caroline Carmichael. And it was that love, love in the service of two young lives that threatened to uncover her deception. That was when she came to me. And that was when I decided to help.

I would like to add the following note to the above report: it is the record of a conversation that I had with Martha Sedgewick one afternoon after Heidi had demanded to be kidnapped and after the plans for her rehabilitation had been made.

Martha began by telling me that the money had never been an important factor in her decision to assume the identity of Caroline Carmichael.

"I find that hard to believe," I said.

"Oh," she answered, "the money is nice because it represents margins."

"Margins?"

"Yes, margins. Margins of time: no rushing, being able to have someone pick up the details. Margins of time and margins of space: large rooms, ample wardrobe, not having to match your wardrobe with the laundry schedule. That's what money buys. The money was important because it bought a certain ease. But I could see that for Winston and Heidi, the money bought too wide a margin. It bought a moat. Grace was able to hide her daughter in Carmichael castle and pull up the drawbridge. The castle was self-contained. And

Grace, using the fear of another kidnapping as an excuse, and using the name of protectiveness was able to widen the margins between Heidi and the world. Unfortunately, Winston was locked in with his sister. Grace called it a margin of safety; it was too ugly to be called by its real name."

"What name would you give it?" I asked.

She shook her head slowly and whispered, "Shame. I'd call it *shame*. Grace was so ashamed of her daughter."

thirteen

I PUT the file down. While I had been reading, Heidi had been working at her desk, she had even dictated something to her secretary, but I don't know what. "How long have you had this?" I asked.

"A long time. I knew that Miss Agatha Trollope held the answers. I always suspected that the famous yellow envelope contained test scores. I had certainly been tested enough to know that psychological tests are as sure an identification as fingerprints. After Father died, and I took over running the corporation, I approached Miss Trollope with a business proposition. I would endow Finchley with a Fine Arts Building, named in her honor, if she would give me information on Caroline. I assured her that I would do nothing to endanger Caroline's position with the family. I told her that, after all, I had other ways to get at the truth. (I didn't really.) And I played on her fondness for Finchley."

"Had you ever confronted Caroline?"

"No. Never. I owed her too much."

"Ever tell Mother?"

"No."

"Why have you never told Mother?"

"Part of the war zone. There is a part of me, Winston, that can never forgive her for being ashamed of me. For allowing me to develop bad manners and bad habits so that they could provide her subconscious with visible evidence that I needed to be hidden, just as the Caroline kidnapping provided her with conscious excuses. Part of me can never forgive her for that. She would have kept me a golliwog."

I thought about what she said. The pain that she felt as she said it was visible. I thought about the pain she must have felt when she had first realized the truth. "Tell her now," I said, half-teasingly, half-sincerely. "Think of the sweetness of revenge. Think how incensed Mother will be when she realizes that the Heidi/Hilary miracle was worked by an impostor."

"I'll not tell her. Now or ever."

"Command decision?" I asked.

"Decision-making is what I am best suited for."

"How lucky for us and for the business that you are. Just think," I said, laughing, "were it not for you, it would have been me taking over when Father died."

"Yes, Winston, dear Winston, with all your talents for literature and learning, you are not suited to business. I am a good provider. In that sense, Mother owes Caroline her way of life, too. Her life in the Club and on committees."

"Give me back the envelope," I said. She handed it to me. I put it inside the manilla folder.

"What are you going to do with them?"

"I am going to the funeral home to make the arrangements, and I am going to very gently and very lovingly place them under my other sister's head. She deserves to be buried with some funny papers, the final frames of our comic strip."

"I'll come with you," Heidi said. "We are her heirs, you know. Just think, at the cost of a small piece of a very large inheritance, I bought a productive life."

"You are a mystery, Heidi," I said. "To have had this file all these years."

"The difference between us, Winston, the difference that makes me an executive and you a writer, is that I have to work from knowing and you have to work from not knowing. That is why I had the open file and that is why you had the sealed envelope."

I studied her, my admiration boundless. "You are mysterious, Hilary Carmichael. Arcane."

"Arcane?"

"Yes, *arcane*. I'm the writer. I can call you that." I tucked her hand in the crook of my arm and held the manilla folder in the other. "Now let us bury Caroline, and Martha Sedgewick with her." We started out of the room. "Because of her," I said, "you lead the life you do, and because you lead the life you do, I can lead the life I do." I stopped just short of the door I was to open. "I guess I owe her two lives."

Judy Blume

knows about growing up. She has a knack for going right to the heart of even the most secret problems and feelings. You'll always find a friend in her books —like these, from YEARLING: